LET ME OUT I'VE HAD ENOUGH

BY

MARK MATTHEWS

Wicked Run Press

"The wicked run when no one is chasing them"
Proverbs 28:1

Wicked Run Press
Let Me Out I've Had Enough is a work of fiction. Names, characters, corporations, institutions, organizations, events or locales in this novel are either the product of the author's imagination or, if real, used fictitiously. Any resemblance to actual persons (living or dead) is entirely coincidental.

For more information, contact: WickedRunPress@gmail.com

Cover Art by Kiren Bagchee

Table of Contents

Welcome to my first published collection of shorts. Just a few words before we start. Most of these stories have never been published. The few which have been published before have been given some nips and tucks and a bit more shine.

Inside you'll find dark works with speculative elements. A couple of stories that could be labeled sci-fi, most that would be labeled horror. Despite their differences, certain things unite them all. In each of work, there is a clear sense of desperation, and when this desperation gets too much, a cry out for help, a plea for relief, a *Let Me Out I've Had Enough.*

This line was partly inspired from that Queen and David Bowie collaborative song, *Under Pressure*, and the lyric: "It's the terror of knowing what this world is about, watching some good friend scream 'let me out'"

Consider this a content warning, for in each story, suicide is portrayed in some fashion. Sometimes it's in the first sentence, sometimes it's at the end, sometimes it's a primary theme, other times it's only a minor element, but you'll find someone wanting to take their own life in every tale. This collection is certainly not meant as some treatise on suicide, but perhaps more for my own therapy. In my profession as a licensed professional counselor, I am exposed to suicide daily, and I think it affects me more than I realize. I estimate I hear of 20 suicide attempts a week, which adds up to over a thousand a year. The idea of life been so terrifying, depressing, debilitating that it becomes unbearable is one of the greatest terrors. Lack of meaning, lack of hope. To want to die.

Dark stuff, right?

I've always felt that talking about our worst fears and most hidden thoughts actually makes us feel lighter, more understood, and therefore eases the weight we all carry. Not being *afraid to go there* is true in both fiction and counseling. Not being *afraid to go there* is true for both writers and therapists. When working with someone who has suicidal ideation, if the mental health clinician is afraid to use the word *suicide* or talk about it openly, this actually can make those who suffer feel more isolated. There's a sense of, "My God, what I'm experiencing is so damn scary my therapist can't even talk about it? Well, I better not talk about it either. I'm so troubled, my darkness can't be penetrated by the healing light of therapy."

This fiction tries to showcase some of that darkness. To shine the light on it and present things we know are there but don't often see. Of course, this work is not for everybody, and I would hate for someone's world to be made more difficult to navigate by reading, so therefore the content warning.

While most of my stories, both within and outside this collection, are considered dark, this is certainly not how I feel about my life. I think others would agree that I'm generally happy, cheerful, perhaps too sarcastic, perhaps too many dad jokes that fall flat, but imagine if I couldn't stick a knife in my heart and spill it all over the page? It's a fantastic outlet.

I find that dark fiction unites us, understands us. Or at least, it understands me, when it's at its best and not afraid to talk about anything, take me to any dark place. Fiction holds my hand while I have a look, and returns me back in a more understood place.

There have been moments in my most despondent days of addiction where I felt, as the title suggests, *Let me out I've had enough*. Well, *I've stayed in*, and I'm so happy I did, for I've felt moments of joy that I never thought possible. I wish that upon everybody who has experienced such hopeless and helplessness, for I like to believe everyone has better days that await, but damn does it require superpowers of patience and perseverance.

Fiction by itself, either writing or reading, is certainly no substitute for real therapy, of which I am an advocate of. I have seen a therapist for many years off and on. It's been said that there are two primary groups who are in therapy—those most mentally fit, (for they are not afraid to deal with their issues) and those most mentally ill—for without therapy, something more disastrous would happen. Sometimes you go from one group to the other.

For free and confidential support for people in distress, or their loved ones, contact the National Suicide Prevention Lifeline at 800-273-8255, text TALK to 741741, or visit https://suicidepreventionlifeline.org.

A few words about each story:

Mastectomy Scars.

This short story first appeared in Shock Totem, when the magazine started a rebirth that unfortunately never seemed to take hold. I'm hoping this work gets a little more traction. It's driven by a concept that people who think of suicide often have the devastating belief that others would prefer them dead.

Body of Christ

As a short novella, it is the longest work you'll find inside. Probably the most strange, but there is more truth here than you might believe. It's not meant as a statement against Christianity as much as rewrite of the resurrection story.

The Last Bug-Chaser

Imagine an alien has come to earth, and rather than quarantine, they need to contract the virus to save the human race, a species that at times seems not worth saving. Written during the pandemic.

Mask of Sanity

Maybe the most *fun* of all the works—depending on what you call *fun*—yet at the same time, the most disturbing.

Tattooed all in Black

His wife is in hospice, but promises to communicate from the afterlife after she passes. Instead, after she dies, he can find no sign, and the loneliness is killing him. This story is inspired by the song *Black* by Pearl Jam. Knowing the song well is hardly a pre-requisite, but feel free to hum the song as you read.

Burdens of the Father

This work first appeared in a charity anthology, Dark Tides, and I'll share to anyone who will listen that it sits on a table of contents alongside Stephen King and Neil Gaiman. A day at the park in a dystopian world of environmental nightmares.

Howling from the Gallows

This story takes place in the realm of my novel, *The Hobgoblin of Little Minds*. Having read the novel first gives some backstory, but it's written to be serve as a stand-alone story. It takes place after Maya has left the psychiatric hospital. The first chapter of The Hobgoblin of Little Minds is available at the end of this collection.

Met My Old Lover in the Grocery Store

I wrote this as the back story to one of my favorite Christmas songs, that melancholy tune, *Same Old Lang Syne* by Dan Fogelberg. Once again, knowing the song not a requirement. Placed here as the final story for a reason that hopefully will reveal itself when the time comes.

Thank you! The best introductions fade in comparison to the words that follows, so these sentences have vanished as I take you by the hand. *Poof*

MASTECTOMY SCARS

"Your therapist won't stop you from killing yourself. You know that, right?" Dad said to Mom. "You're going to do it if you really want to."

And she did.

I found my mom in the bathtub after I came home from rehearsal on a Tuesday night. The play was Hamlet and I was cast as Ophelia, but Mom seemed to be playing the role. Her eyes were open, and she looked up to the ceiling while her body lay motionless in the water. The bath was a cold, murky red swamp.

I don't think my dad knew he would be right when he said those words, but they had ended their fight before Dad raised a fist and mom retreated to her room as always. This time, she responded by opening up her veins and drowning in a mix of water and blood, her insides turned out.

I was alone in the house when I found her. I didn't scream. I didn't break out in tears. I wished I had. I wished my own heart had burst and I had bled out and fell right next to her. Instead, I watched her float. I pictured white daffodils, like little boats, floating next to her, and imagined her lips curled into a content smile. The rest of her frail, tired body looked like an alien preserved in formaldehyde, the mastectomy scars like old battle wounds. A razor and empty brown prescription bottle lay on the bathroom floor. She had cut her veins, she had taken an overdose.

She hadn't let the cancer kill her.

They put a black wig on her head before laying her out at the funeral home. The wig was a much darker pitch then her hair had ever been, and I hated they tried to hide her scalp. Placing my hand on mom's bald head had always helped me connect with her, as if I could feel the thoughts squirming underneath. Even after putting a knit cap on her head, she had so often felt cold, so I would lie next to her. My warm skin pressed against her cold and dying flesh was a human radiator. I thought of doing the same in the casket, but this wasn't her anymore, despite the thick makeup meant to make her look alive, she was gone. Her fingers were folded over each other in eternal contemplation, but the wedding ring had been taken off her finger.

Those who came to visit in their suits and dresses talked about the *cancer*. Only the *cancer*. Not that she had killed herself. *Dakota, please keep this private.* It was the cancer that killed her, so please donate to find a cure.

Flowers lined the room at the wake, brought in by tall, lanky funeral home workers. I said awkward words to people I barely knew. Their faces were fake, and so was mine. Nobody could see my real hurt. The pain inside was eating at my spine, like tiny piranhas, frenetically devouring my organs and drinking my spinal fluid. I didn't let it show, and the whispering people who kept glancing my way said I was brave.

As the priest spoke his words, I squeezed my eyes shut and made sure not to cry. Kate, my dad's friend from work, stood by his side while holding his hand. She wore a deep purple dress that made her seem proud of the cancer-free breasts lying underneath.

I was right outside the somber, funeral home bathroom when I saw my mom's therapist. I recognized her from the two therapy sessions mom had taken me to so I could *prepare for the passing.* Tears had puddled inside her eyes, her face was a mess, and she kept making sniffing noises again and again.

She looked at me with surprise, gave a huge sniff of her nose, and stood up to give me a hug. I hugged her back and my body crumbled. I feared she'd rip a hole inside me for everyone to see.

"Why?" I whispered with my mouth pressed into her.

The squeeze grew tighter. I didn't want it to end.

"I wish I knew. I wish I had an answer. It wasn't for lack of love, but perhaps because of too much. But you'll never be alone. Her blood will be in your veins always."

My dad's friend Kate had a different answer a week later.

"Your mom was being thoughtful when she killed herself," Kate said. "It is sad, but she knew it was time to move on. For her. For us. It is tragic, but there are worse things coming."

The house was put up for sale so we could *start fresh*, and Kate had been cleaning behind spots that had never been cleaned before. The whole house smelled like sour lemon Windex.

"Your mom would understand why your dad has to get on with his life, why we have to show the house. Your dad needs my help, so I'll be here a lot."

Kate had already been over a lot, visiting Dad while Mom was gone seeing doctors, shopping, or just lying in bed with such fatigue it seemed she'd never rise. Kate and Dad would sneak downstairs together, and when they came back up, they were out of breath and their clothes were wrinkled. If I was within earshot they said business words loudly meant for me to hear, words meant as their disguise. Words I know they didn't use downstairs.

We staged the house, I had to leave. I went to watch the final dress rehearsals for Hamlet. I'd dropped out of my role and hovered above things. Outside of things. A mannequin to others, just wearing clothes and taking up space, but when I was alone, I cried with hurt. My stomach felt like it was bleeding, my chest cavity like it was full of knives slicing it apart. The marrow of my soul had a pain so hidden it could never heal, so I lay in bed with hands wrapped around my neck, spine curled around the pain, trying to embrace myself but finding no relief.

And always alone.

It wasn't my heart that pumped my blood anymore, it was a ball of razor-sharp hurt. I couldn't take it, so I finally asked my Dad if I could see Mom's therapist. The therapist had secrets that I needed to hear.

"No. No way," he answered. "She made your mom worse. Mom was already damaged goods, but that therapist broke her entirely."

When my dad spoke like that, with his head to the ground as if making a pact with the devil, with muscles clenching and his blue jugular pulsating in his neck, I knew enough to accept his response and move on before he got up from his chair and started pounding on things.

But Kate hadn't learned these rules, and made a soft plea. "Maybe she should see the therapist? It could really help us if she did. She should follow in the footsteps of her mom."

It was left unanswered, but Kate approached me later in private. She sat bedside, pulled her blonde hair behind her ear, and spoke with cotton softness.

"You miss your mom, don't you?" she asked. "I am sure you can't stop thinking about her killing herself like that. In fact, you may have been thinking about doing the same thing that your mom did. It's only natural. The sadness must be unbearable. Of course you should see this therapist. It is very important you talk about things like your mother did, see how she felt, do what she did."

Kate made the therapy appointment and wrote it on the calendar as *Mani-Pedi date w/Dakota* to disguise it from my dad.

Kate spent the night. Often. She slept over so many days in a row that soon enough she was moved in. The smell of my mom's cancer that had been stuck to the walls like paint just days ago was being replaced with the scent of my dad's new flower. She cooked my dad's favorite meals and spoke to me about how sad I must be feeling. "I know you're hurt and lonely dear, don't pretend you're not. You'll see your mom again. You're just like her."

I wished I could see Mom soon, or at least feel her in our house. To hear the floorboards creak from her slow, cancerous gait, to know the place was still haunted by her soul. Instead, the house got filled with Kate's stuff. Yoga pants and bras in the dyer, shampoo in the shower, everything in its place, except she always left her Lady Bic razor on the bathroom counter. It greeted me each morning, said good night to me each night, like Kate herself needed to intrude on the most solitary room in my house.

When I glanced in the bathroom mirror, I longed to see mom's body lying in the tub behind me, even if she was just dead and lying there in the bloody red water. Until then, I was alone and staring at myself, nobody aware of the hurt that drove me to tears, the aches of being chewed apart by an infestation in my gut.

The pain of being alive without my mom was making my insides bleed.

Why didn't I just lock the bathroom door when I found her in the tub? I could have laid down next to her in the water until someone busted down the door and took us both away.

The Lady Bic seemed as lonely as I, so I picked it up off the bathroom counter. It was light in my hand, a tiny magic wand that could make people vanish to other worlds. I pressed it gently against the blue vein of my wrist as if using the blade to take my pulse. My heart beat louder, faster, the tiny bits inside scurrying as if a door was about to open, and for once, I felt a peace, as if they had stopped chewing at my spine.

I put the razor down. The contents of my veins flowed as normal, shooting along their tunnel just below the skin, unencumbered. But even with the razor gone, the sharp bites returned, but hotter, like each new wound bleeding inside me had to be cauterized by a searing flame.

I searched the cabinet and found one of mom's many prescription bottles, still there as if waiting for her return. For a moment I imagined emptying all the Vicodin's into my hand, but instead dotted out just two, like tic-tacs, tap-tap. I popped them into my mouth and chewed them up so they would work faster. How hard might it be to swallow more?

I ran the bathwater, and then looked in the mirror and used the razor to shave my head. The first cut took off a lock of my short, spiky hair that fell to the sink, drifting like a leaf from a tree. More black hair followed and gathered on the floor. I hacked through the locks down to the scalp, and once it was short enough, lathered my head with shaving cream and shaved it all off. All that remained were dozens of razor cuts on my bald head. I rubbed my hand over my work, fingers trembling, drops of blood from razor burns on my fingers, and I stared unblinking into the mirror. A snake who had shed her skin, and proud of it.

Bald as my mom.

I loved the first step into the bath. The scolding water turned my white flesh to red as I lay down. I imagined Kate lying in this same spot, shaving her legs, breasts floating in the water.

They were un-diseased, un-ravaged by radiation or chemotherapy. My dad had discarded a breastless woman with mastectomy scars for a new, younger specimen, but Kate had no idea of what was below his surface.

I let myself sink into the bath, my eyes just above the surface, my ears just beneath the water so I could hear the underworld. The shaving nicks on my head were burning, but the pain felt good, a sweet relief. I wasn't sure if it was from the Vicodin or the warm rush of the water around me, but I felt like a fetus again, protected in a warm womb, and soon enough, I heard the voice of my mother.

She wants you to kill yourself, you know that, right?

I didn't answer, for it couldn't really be her.

She wants you to kill yourself, Mom repeated.

Her voice was in that tone she'd use hours after a violent argument with dad and she would emerge from her room, somber and serious.

"What should I do? I need you with me." I answered

My words moved below the surface like a sonic wave, and I had to wait for a response to bounce back.

Do what she asks of you.

"I can't. I am scared. Scared of everything."

I know. I was scared too.

 "Why? Why did you kill yourself? Why did you do it?"

I had to release what I was holding inside. I had to let my insides out. I couldn't take it anymore. The pain, the hurt. I took my life. Took it elsewhere. You should do the same.

"What do I do?"

Cut yourself. You have razors ripping at your insides anyways, I know this, and if you don't let it out, it will kill you just the same. Cut yourself. Do it, sweetie, cut yourself.

Cut yourself.

I stood up and stepped on the bathmat, reached for Kate's Lady Bic with one hand, and the bottle of Vicodin in the other. I stepped back into the bath, and the hot water invited me inside to stay. I opened up the Vicodin bottle, poured pills into my mouth, and grinded them in my teeth. I swallowed hard and felt them go down. I imagined them softening the thousand slashes I felt on my spine, and soon, the slashes on my wrist.

I pressed the Bic against my vein.

That's it, sweetie. Relief is coming.

It didn't hurt when I pressed down and slashed sideways, it just stung with an electric zap and a current that ran up my spine. I took a deep breath, and watched as a crowd of red rushed out of the small exit in my wrist, gathered in a red mass, and then went streaming down my arm. It swirled into the water, tiny crimson tornados.

I changed hands with the razor and sliced my other wrist. Another army of red started their match out of my body and into the bathwater.

It began to pour, only it wasn't my blood anymore, but an army of scurrying red ants with chewing mandibles and body segments fattened from feeding on my spine. I saw for the first time what before I had only felt, what had driven me to tears. They were hungry for blood, eager for something new, wanted to *start fresh.* As the red ants left me the relief from pain was exquisite, a soothing lullaby, the sound of Vicodin, cradled in bliss. The horde of red insects swirled down the drain, through the veins of the house, down into the same spot my mother's insides were, deep within the bowels of our home.

There was shock on my dad's face when he saw me the next morning. I figured he would not approve of my shaved head. His mouth shot open in surprise, then closed in anger, teeth clenched so that his jaw bones trembled. He saw me truly for the first time at that moment laying in the tub, and I could feel his thoughts—*You were too odd for me to understand. You, your mom, my own mom. All of you scared the hell out of me and all I can do is pummel the walls with my fists.*

The pain was gone, my dad was somber, and Kate did what she does—diligently cleaned the house, bleached what she could, mopped everywhere she could reach, cooked each night, and spent more time on her hair. On at least one occasion, she put on a black dress that dipped low and exposed her breasts, went to a formal event, and then came home and boxed my books. The therapy appointment, disguised as *Mani-Pedi date w/Dakota* was crossed off the calendar without explanation.

My dad's rage built in silence, a pressure that I knew so well but Kate couldn't detect. The house was so quiet at night I could hear the patter of my mom's feet, same way I heard them as a child, coming to place a warm palm on my cheek and wake me for school.

The silence and stillness of the house was finally interrupted when the realtor called. *We got an offer on the house!* Kate danced with glee, my dad was reluctant to join, but Kate assured him that it all happened at the perfect time after so much bad luck.

She started packing, but memories of mom and I would not be taken to the new house, we'd remain deep in the bowels, haunting it from below the surface, like dust never cleaned until it soaks into the place and is forgotten. But the celebration stopped after Dad finished a long phone call full of venomous words.

"The deal is off," he told Kate as soon as it ended, "the purchase didn't go, the offer is pulled."

"What? You're joking. What happened?"

"Didn't pass the house inspection. We have termites. Red termites eating up the wood. Load bearing walls are shit. We need major repairs, have to pull the listing. Our realtor refuses to list it *as is*."

Kate tucked her blonde hair behind her ear as if she hadn't heard him correctly.

"No. We'll get someone else. We need someone else to do the home inspection. I have a guy I know."

"Didn't you hear me? Off the market. Terrible case of a rare breed of red termites. It's done. We're screwed."

Dad paced, with each step getting angrier, looking to the heavens for energy to keep going. He always found it.

"You come in here and think you know shit?" He yelled at Kate. "You think I don't know the right people? That's why you are here, to get a piece of *what I know*. Well, here's what I do know…"

The vein in his neck bulged into a snake ready to burst out of his neck. His fists cocked back, and he slammed it into the wall, first making one hole, and then an identical hole just a few feet aside—bamn, bamn—letting Kate know *this could be your skull getting smashed in.* She had seen the face of the stranger, the one my mom had come to fear. A person who drove my mom mad, who didn't go to the radiation appointments or sit bedside, who reminded my mom that other women didn't need a therapist who went through this. That most woman gave their man a son, not just a knock-off daughter and smaller version of themselves, so why should he try again to have another child?

And like my mom, Kate scurried with fear to her room.

I stayed in the empty silent space, eyes drawn to the gaping holes my dad had just cut open. The dry wall was splintered into jagged pieces. Two, big bloody wounds, and as if the house itself was begging to be cut open and offered relief, the insides started spilling out. Tiny bits puddled near the openings, and then dripped down the walls. A stream of tiny red ants, termites, really, with mandibles sharp as razors, poured out of the wounds. The trail of them, like one moving organism with a million parts, walked across the wood floor. I could hear the pitter of their feet, and watched them move like a flame following a trail of gas. They went directly to the bedroom Kate had retreated to, and I followed. They slipped under the door, these tiny creatures I knew so well, and I pushed the door open to bear witness.

The termites had already moved up the bedposts and covered Kate's body. Her clothes whittled to ash in an instant by the time she woke up and began to flail about, a body on fire and just as defenseless. Her fingers dug at her eyes since her eyelids were quickly digested and the insects were free to eat the pupil beneath. Soon she was blind, scratching at her bloody skin in a stupor.

I watched as if seeing my own insides from just days ago brought to life before me. I remember each incision, each sting. I knew if I put one of them under a microscope, I would not be surprised to see them eye to eye, for I've come to know them well.

But the invaders were not from me alone, for I could smell the cancer again. My insides had joined with mom's, our veins split open and the fluids joined forces, and now the creatures ravaged Kate's body.

The agony became too much, and Kate finally fell back to the bed in defeat, her flesh tissue nearly gone, her body alive but fading. Like infants, the creatures fed at her breasts, devouring them, whittling down the mounds to nothing, decomposing her chest while Kate lay still as any patient would while receiving a full mastectomy.

I stood watch as if at a wake, watching her die, and I felt mom next to me, holding my hand same as Kate had held the hand of my dad.

Only in this wake, the body would be eaten. Eaten down to the bone.

The rush, the swirl, the screams—all of it built until my dad came rushing into the room. The fear in his eyes was nothing like the blank face he had at mom's funeral. His flower had been killed, eaten by all the misery trapped inside this house and set free.

Kate's body began to move. It sat upright from the bed and got on its feet. Whether Kate was still alive inside the swarm, or if the insects themselves had taken human shape, I wasn't sure, but she stood tall before my dad and spread her arms for an embrace. Every bit of her was covered in movement, just tiny red dots crawling and scurrying over one another.

My dad shook in fear. The blue vein in his neck, the red pitch of his anger, his hammer fists, all of them were gone, instead, his face grew pale when his flower embraced him. She held his body and they swayed in a seductive dance, to and fro, softly to music only they could hear. Soon, the red termites crawled onto his arm and scurried onto his body. They covered his face and went up his nostrils to his brain. They moved under his eyelids to his eyeball. They swirled inside his ear canals. They frantically marched into his slack jaw which hung open in shock.

The termites were no longer eating, but filling themselves inside a new host.

Getting *a fresh start.*

In the silence of the house in the days that followed, I could hear them feeding off his spine, his gut, his organs. Dad was being eaten alive from the inside out, alone inside a house with two wounds that wouldn't heal, just mastectomy scars from a fight with cancer.

I waited for the day Dad had to open himself up for relief from the pain.

BODY OF CHRIST

Chapter One: Faith

THE PLASTIC MASK over Mom's nose made Faith think of her as a fighter pilot, ready to fly to the heavens and do battle.

Not as a patient lying in a hospital bed.

"She isn't in there anymore," her dad said, squeezing Faith's fingers with each syllable as if trying to pump out a response.

Faith didn't want to reply. Mom wasn't a *brain*—she was a heart, and that was still beating; she was a spirit, and that was still living. Didn't matter she was in a "hopelessly vegetative state" underneath those snow-white bedsheets.

Faith kept watch by the hospital bed and waited for mom's eyelids to flutter. Any minute now the pupil underneath would show itself like a golden sunrise on a sandy beach.

Mom loves the beach.

"The doctors feel it's best to say our goodbyes," her dad said. "Your mom is being kept alive by machines. The doctors can't fix what happened. She'll never be the same."

Tears welled inside Faith's head, hot lava in a volcano, her brain felt ready to blow. She'd been holding it in ever since her mom had gone missing overnight. After the call came saying Mom's Toyota was found crashed in the ravine, everything was supposed to be okay. They rushed to the hospital to find Mom unconscious. Broken bones were wrapped in casts, and her face was cut and bruised. One side of her head had to be shaven in order for them to stitch it back together.

Three straight days they came to watch over her, waiting for her to wake. Her dad made calls, wrote down numbers, gave hugs to guests, and each day had private talks with doctors.

The private talks ended after her dad made his decision and the doctor's recommendation was set into motion.

"It takes a while to break the equipment down," said the doctor. "Families find it best to leave the room for a moment while we take care of things. Just a few minutes."

Pulling the plug wasn't so easy after all.

The machines weren't keeping her alive, it was her spirit. They'd soon find out.

They left room 364 to a well-lit hall. Faith walked by the nurses' station, and her favorite nurse winked.

See, they know the secret. Mom's not going to die.

They walked to the sitting room where chairs lined the walls and a woman sat nervously, purse on her lap, head swiveling to each side as if afraid to miss something. On the ground her son was pushing a plastic toy car along carpet, passing time in his own way.

This is where people come waiting for others to die.

Her dad paced back and forth as Faith watched, sure that he was coming up with a plan to make things better. This was all a terrible mistake, a fixable error they'd laugh about in years to come. Dad was thinking, and each step he took he got him closer to the answer. But before he could find the solution, a nurse came and whispered in his ear.

They went back to room 364 and there her mom was, lying without the pilot mask over her face. The tubes had been removed, hanging from the equipment like dead tentacles. It was just Mom, sleeping, without medical equipment to weigh her down.

She was ready to rise.

Faith knew secrets that the men in white suits didn't understand. They never witnessed the golden halo that surrounded Mom when she prayed at church. Never heard her spirit hum, or how her singing chimed like the church bells. Mom took communion with such grace you could feel her spirit vibrate, and with each praise of *hallelujah* everyone was a little less cold and a lot less broken. Hers was a spirit they could not put down.

Faith crouched beside the bed, watching her mom fight to get back to life. Her chest was rising, falling, rising, falling, rising, failing.

"She's still breathing. She's breathing harder," Faith told the doctor, ready to add *I told you so.*

"She's struggling for air," said the doctor. "Her heart is slowing. Her lungs will soon stop. She will go peacefully and not suffer one bit, but we can't be certain how long it will take. Best that you two be left alone. Please come get me if you have questions."

It may take a while, Faith agreed silently, because she's not dying. Not today. Soon her eyes would open and she'd rise from the bed after enduring her three days of hospital hell. Medical staff would gather. Happy tears would flow. Mom often surprised her with a glass of orange juice on the bed stand to wake her up—today she would surprise everyone, and be reborn.

Faith put her hand over her mom's knuckle. It was warm in the palm of her hand.

Mom, if you can hear me, let them know you're in there. That you're alive. That you're coming home. Open your eyes. Open your eyes.

Faith waited for the response, and soon enough, she could feel a shift. Something stirred underneath, a slight twitch of her lips, brain waves beneath the purple bruises.

Please God, I need your help. Open her eyes. You can't let her die like this. Lord, hear my prayer.

Faith studied her mom's face. One side was deformed with puffy purple bruises bulging from her skin. The other side was soft and fair, only slightly weathered with wrinkles. Locks of hair, stringy from salt water swims, covered half her head. She was an ocean goddess.

Mom. Please. Make a noise. Open your eyes.

Then the noise came. So soft that her lips didn't move, but a noise nonetheless. Faith took a deep breath. Her muscles tensed, her ears straining, trying to hear it again.

More sounds came, faint, but growing louder, building, until they became a desperate cry for help. A siren's wail on a dark night.

Faith winced. The noise cut into her ears like slivers of glass slashing at her ear drums. She wanted to cover her head and block the noise but needed to hear her mom's screams.

Because then they changed to words. The piercing scream for help turned to something Faith could understand.

Don't let me die. My life is precious. Save me, Faith. I am here.

"Hook her back up, Dad. Bring her back," Faith pleaded.

Her dad stepped forward and tried to hug Faith but she pushed him away.

Faith. I am here. Inside here.

"Get the doctor, we need to save her. She's still alive."

"Yes, Faith, she is still alive," her dad said. "You'll want to hug her…one last time."

Faith did hug her. She laid her body across her mom's, burrowing into her, waiting to feel her mother's embrace. The spirit below longed to hold Faith but could not. The doctor had turned the body off, the spirit had to leave.

FAITH. I AM HERE. INSIDE HERE.

The words climbed to a pitch so frantic they were no longer understood but just one long cry of agony. The shriek of a banshee, a dying soul being buried alive, wondering why her family was standing there, letting her die, as if they were the ones who'd run her off the road, over the guard rail, and into the rock-filled ravine below.

> *WHY*
>   *HAVE*
>   *YOU*
>   *ABANDONED*
>   *ME?*

These words echoed through her mom's body and slowly faded as if she were falling down a well. Her heartbeat stopped. The chest that had been rising and falling went completely still. Faith stared at her mom's face, waiting for a miracle, for the eyelids to rise, but instead the jaw had gone slack. The color of life was gone. Only pale, cold colors were left. Faith's own cries came next, but like the voice of her dying mother, the pitch too high for her dad to hear. Her pain remained hidden.

Visiting the funeral parlor and seeing her Mom's body lying in the casket gave Faith an aching pain in her gut. Bile rose up her throat and she swallowed back down the bitter taste. She made tiny prayers to Jesus to take away her grief and embrace her mom's soul. She prayed so hard she expected Jesus to answer.

But nothing came.

Life was like a limb gone numb and Faith dragged along for the weeks that followed. She'd stare out the front window of her house, watching the boy across the street, Keagan, and his father, walk to the church that butted up to the end of their street to play baseball. She envied the boy and longed for time with one of her own parents, but her dad was so distant, his spirit so dim. His emotions were in a vegetative state and unhooked from machines that kept them alive.

Colors in the house started to fade. Dust in the air seemed to rise up in clouds, more and more with each passing day, suspended in streaks of sunlight. Her sheets were never as clean as before; she missed the scent of lilacs on her pillowcase—sweet, but heavy with vanilla—and feeling like she was like Eve sleeping in the garden.

The orange juice was full of thick pulp that stuck in her teeth. Church felt lonely no matter who was standing next to her. The flowers on her dress wilted.

The day that Faith had her first period there was not a woman to be found in her house. There were only memories of her mom that hung in Faith's mind and had to be dusted off or else they'd be forgotten. The memory of Mom describing her first period would forever remain a vivid one:

I was lying in the surf, tasting salt water on my tongue and watching the whitecaps roll up my belly, bubble under my chin, and then roll back down, leaving me there to sparkle under the sun. I clutched on to handfuls of sand, once in a while watching a tiny shell creature burrowing for cover. I noticed a thin twirl of red between my legs. I wasn't scared or shocked, just curious, a fortunate witness to something miraculous. I laid there for as long as I could, watching the blood swirl from my bathing suit, and after a while I could hear the heartbeat of the egg: boop-boop, boop-boop, ever so faint, and I knew it was ridiculous, but I could hear it nonetheless. I could sense it when the tiny egg swam away, fueled by the ocean waves pulling it back to sea. The egg was off to join the rest of the living, as if the nutrients of the ocean would care for it and help it grow. This is what happens. As a woman, we give birth to life every month. Our blood is like the ocean water that fuels living things.

Faith wished she were somewhere majestic like her mom was when she got her first period, instead of being locked in the bathroom, standing on cold tiles, looking into the sink where her dad's used razor was still frothy with cream. Dead bits of his stubble dotted the sink.

Her menses just started, but her underwear was more than just spotted. It was wet with sticky-red blood. The bathroom mirror mocked her, reflecting back the lost look on her face, reminding her that she was all alone with nobody to count on.

She folded up her bloody underwear, wrapped it thick with toilet paper, and placed it in the garbage. She opened the flowery pastel wrapper and inserted the pad into a clean pair of underwear, same way she'd practiced many times over during false alarms. She wondered if her dad would notice what was in the bathroom garbage and come wake her up, the way her mom most certainly would have done, rather than just stay in his room doing his secret things.

She decided to tell him. He needed to know she was changed.

The door to his room was cracked, and she pushed it all the way open. She missed the way the scent of her mom's hairspray and perfume would greet her.

"Daddy?" she asked. It seemed right to call him *daddy* at that moment, but there was no answer. He was in the corner on his computer desk, headphones wrapped around his ears.

"Daddy. I need to tell you something. It happened."
Nothing

"It happened," she said louder, expecting him to ask, *what was IT?* since a dad wouldn't know what *IT* was, like a mom would.

Dad didn't respond. He didn't hear. She felt like a ghost, invisible, watching him. She waited for him to sense her presence, but nothing. She thought about tapping him on the back and explaining what happened, but he wouldn't know what to do or what to say, so she slipped back out, still unnoticed, and went to bed.

The night was restless. Cramps in her gut came and went, then came back stronger. The Stayfree pad seemed to grow in size and she couldn't forget it was there. She would turn on the light to check, changed the pad more than once, and became worried maybe this wasn't how it was supposed to happen. *I'm going to bleed out forever, and nobody will know, not a mom to help me.* Fears pinballed inside her head; zip-zapping neurons, zooming fast and then popping. Blood seeped from the cracks. Every new moment a new wound bleeding. She was open to the world now, ready to create life, and life started to roll in. Dark waves from a cold ocean, each one more frigid, rushing over her head so that she had to gasp for breath. She was sure she was going to drown in her sleep until the ocean shattered like ice and she heard a cry for help.

Why
have
you
abandoned
me?

The same scream as her mom's, but not her mom's voice. It was someone else, mocking her.

She forced her eyes open so that the dream would stop, but the real world was just as cold and dark, and the scream remained, just as strong.

Why have you abandoned me?

The sound wasn't coming from her dream, it was coming from inside the house. Somewhere outside her bedroom the noise was gaining power. Each pitch climbed higher with the urgency of a smoke alarm. With hands over ears and a hazy brain she got up from her bed and dashed from her bedroom, heading right into the eye of the hurricane, the center of the noise that threatened to shatter her skull.

Why
Have
You
Abandoned me?

It was loudest in the bathroom and she went inside, her ears trying to detect the source of the strongest signal.

The cry was erupting from the garbage. She reached inside, fished the wrapped-up remnants of her menses and held it to her ear. The blast of noise made her cheeks wilt.

WHY HAVE YOU ABANDONED ME?

It was the voice of her own egg.

Wrapped in a pile of toilet paper and stuffed in the garbage, the bloody egg was alive and crying out, as if it were an infant, left in a dumpster by a cold, cruel mother.

She rolled the pad in more toilet paper, brought it into her bedroom, and placed it in her pajama drawer. When she changed her next pad, she did the same.

Her dad was sleeping quietly, unaware of the death, the abandonment, the lost life. He couldn't hear the perpetual scream that lived in Faith's brain. Nobody could.

The scream faded a touch over the coming weeks, but came back with rage and vengeance when her next cycle came. She was creating life each month, but then pulling the plug, and letting it die.

<u>Chapter Two: Keagan, the boy from across the street</u>

"Halloween isn't for Christians. Not for real Christians. We don't hand out candy around here, and we don't carve up pumpkins. People who do that are fake Christians, the kind who celebrate Easter with candy, who forget about Holy Thursday and Good Friday. Your dad's a fake Christian, and the Lord snapped him in half for it."

Keagan's dad was snapped in half, his momma was right about that. Every day he moaned in pain from his broken back, then he'd pop open a prescription bottle, cup the pills in his hands like M&Ms, and eat them before they'd melt. At night, he'd cry out in his sleep, and shuffle around the halls, groaning like a ghost. Keagan would stay awake until the moaning stopped and his dad had plopped himself back down in the Lazy-Boy chair.

Dad was in the recliner now, watching Sunday politics, but Mom had gone straight back to bed after getting home from church. She said it was only a sign of the Lord's grace that she was summoned forth to attend Mass on Halloween. Keagan was bringing her a second bowl of Lucky Charms.

"Easter is when Jesus rose from Hell and brought sinners with him. Sinners like you. But it was Good Friday when he was bloodied by a crown of thorns and let nails be pounded through his legs. And on Holy Thursday, that's when he said, 'This is my body,' and had his disciples eat of his flesh, and then drink of his blood."

Keagan flashed a smile and put the cereal bowl down next to the bed, using it to scoot over the cans of Mountain Dew, but the motion caused waves of milk to spill over the edge.

"I'm sorry, Momma."

He stood still, waiting for his punishment, frozen in time, reading Momma's face.

"You're such a rotten sinner. So rotten. Come here."

She held out her arm and hugged him with rolls of dough, cold dough, since the meat that hung off of them was always frigid. Keagan was sucked into her embrace and mushed against her breasts. He was suffocating and closed his eyes, waiting for it to be over.

"You need to eat of Jesus's body. Your time has finally come for a taste of the Eucharist. I know you're scared. I know you're unclean. I know my love, my only love, but you have to do this right or you're lost, you see. Lost. When the priest holds out the wafer and says, 'Body of Christ,' you'd better say 'Amen.' Amen means you agree. It means there is no doubt in your mind that you are eating the Body of Christ. Not something pretend. Not something that makes you *think* of the Body of Christ, or *represents* the Body of Christ, but his very skin right there on your tongue."

"What does it taste like?" Keagan asked, only because he knew Momma wanted to talk more.

"That all depends," she said, and finally let him out of the headlock hug. "If you say Amen and don't mean it, it'll burn your tongue and hurt your stomach. It will poison your insides if you are not worthy. But if you say Amen like you believe Jesus is the son of God, that you are eating His flesh, and that you are worthy of salvation, then it'll taste like a piece of God. It will grow inside you and replace all the bad parts."

"Motherfucker. Motherfucker."

It was the voice of Keagan's dad, cursing either at politics on the TV or because of the pain in his back, it was hard to tell which.

"Go to your dad," his momma said, pushing him away. "Go see him now. Tell him you love him. Tell him. We must love fake Christians. It's our way to give them Communion. We'd feed them all the Body of Christ, if we could."

Keagan obeyed and walked down the hallway to his dad in the dusty brown Lazy-Boy chair. Dad was staring at the TV, so Keagan stared with him, listening to the people talk politics. He tried hard to get mad at what they said but just couldn't. Dad had stopped cussing, but his breathing rattled in his chest. Keagan could feel the whole room expand and shrink with each breath, and even though the noise of his dad's breathing scared him, he hated to think of it stopping.

"I love you, Dad," Keagan said, thinking his dad had fallen asleep, but then his eyelids opened and the familiar white slits appeared. His dad smiled, reached out his arm, and Keagan walked into it and felt it curl around him and wrap him up. Dad's skin smelled like the smoke from the factory he'd worked in years ago. The smell of smoke stuck in his skin and would never shed.

"You don't love me," his dad said, still smiling. "Not like this. You love memories of me. You love that I done carried you on my back, love that I done took you for ice cream, that we sat and watched ball together, done let you do things your mom never would. Only reason I married her after she got pregnant is to protect you from her. But you don't need me no more. I'm done living and goin' to die tonight."

"Tonight?"

"Yes, Keagan. Tonight, I die."

His shaky arm pulled away, but Keagan didn't want to be let go. He wanted to jump in the chair with his dad and watch SportsCenter. Or go back to summers when Dad's back didn't hurt and they'd spend days 'shagging flies' together at St. Mary's baseball field. Instead, he looked down at his shoes. His church shoes that Momma bought him were too big. *He'd grow into them soon enough.*

The arguing men on the politics show stopped. A commercial came on for a cruise line.

"Son, I need you to get me something. In my closet. Way in the back. There's a brown leather box. You got to dig around to find it. Bring it to me. Okay?"

Keagan knew what he meant. He'd seen the box before. Even opened it.

"What do you want that for?"

"Don't make me get up son, come on now."

Keagan had to obey. He went to his dad's closet and dug through the shoes and musty leather belts. He knew where the box was, but took longer to find it, to fake like he didn't know. He loved the box. It made huge snapping noises when you clicked it open and shut.

He retrieved the box and presented it to his dad, who grunted and opened it with a *click*.

The gun was tucked safely inside.

Dad pulled out the gun, turned it side to side, then set it next to his prescription bottle.

"Are you worried about trick-or-treaters tonight?" Keagan asked.

"Son, son, son. I can't barely walk no more, ain't you listening? *I am going to die.* Tonight. World Series is over, I got barb wire for a backbone rippin' up my insides, stabbin' me all over. I'm being tortured each day I stay alive, and I'm begging for it to end."

Keagan didn't know his dad's eyes could still open that wide. Only time they did was when Keagan would lob him pitches at the field, and Dad would take turns smashing tennis balls with his collection of Louisville sluggers. Didn't stop until he hit a shot with all of them, and he never took a swing and missed. Keagan couldn't get a pitch past him.

"Will you see me make my First Holy Communion?"

"Probably not. Can't see such things the place I'm going."

Sadness bubbled from Keagan's gut, boiled up his body, filled his head, and then dripped from his eyes.

"Come on now, I ain't even living no more, and you don't need me, like you don't need no Communion and don't need no Jesus. We all on earth just got to make our own Jesus. Fuck that noise your momma sayin'. She the one that broke me—she won't say so, and it don't matter because she can't help breaking people. I done had enough of this world. You got all I had to give, and nothin' I can do anymore will help."

"But you got doctors."

"Doctors just people, Keagan, just people who hurting, too. Just go, okay. Leave me here. Go. Don't worry, I'm not going to shoot myself. I promise. And I've never made a promise to you that I haven't kept, have I?"

Keagan couldn't think of a single one.

"Good. Now let me take one last nap. I'll rise again, don't worry."

Dad's slitty white eyes closed, and Keagan waited around until his jaw hung slack and he heard wind rustle from his pipes. The gun was right there, Keagan could grab it, but soon as he reached, he knew his dad would wake and grab his wrist.

Keagan walked back to his bedroom and went directly inside his own closet: a big, walk-in closet, and when the door closed, his whole world went pitch dark. No matter how light it was outside, Keagan's closet made things go black. Keagan loved to sit inside, unable to see a thing, the only sound in the world his own heart beating.

The only light inside was a flashlight, the kind with the big square battery, and he'd fastened a blue fabric over top so that when it was turned on, everything was covered as if in the glow of the moon.

The closet was the only place he could really think about things like tasting the flesh of Jesus, like his dad saying he was dying tonight, like the gun sitting next to him. Nobody ever bothered him. Slipping inside was like going back to the place you were before you were born.

On the shelf was a bunch of board games. Monopoly, Risk, Battleship, Stratego. Dotted about the floor were little plastic baggies Keagan always kept on hand to gather things and bring back to his lair. Some had munchies inside, like Cheez-Its or Pringles, another had a worm inside that he'd found writhing around in the sun on the sidewalk covered with a million black ants that it just couldn't squirm away from. The worm had died and grown stale, and the ants had dried up into tiny pieces of dust. Next to the worm was a Ziploc bag full of water that used to be a chunk of snow. Keagan had built a snowman, reached into its chest, pulled out a fist-sized snowball, and pretended it was the snowman's heart. He planned to stick the remains back into the first snowman he built next winter and bring it back to life.

Keagan sat in the dark closet and thought about his dad dying. Hours passed, or minutes. Maybe it was three days or maybe it was three blinks, it was impossible to tell, but he just knew it was time to leave.

He walked out of his room. It was late, the sun nearly down, and outside the chatter of trick-or-treaters. Keagan could tell his momma had been about. She was so big he could still feel the swoosh of the air when she walked to the kitchen and back.

"Momma? Momma?"

She didn't answer, so he gave one louder "Momma?" but nothing.

She was asleep, and when she's asleep, Dad's usually awake. It's how they avoid each other.

Keagan walked to the front room. The front porch light was off, but the shades were still open. Keagan looked across the street and saw his neighbor, Faith, sitting on her front porch, large bowl of candy on her lap. Shadows in the shapes of younger children walked down the sidewalk and up to her porch, bags by their sides.

Keagan's dad was sitting in the recliner watching classic SportsCenter.

"Good. You're back," his dad said. "Time to say goodbye. I'm gonna call now. Goin' to die. You go to your room."

"No, Dad. I don't want you to die."

"Son, I'm done here. You know I'll love you always. Promise me you'll never forget that. And promise me you'll never have a child? It's a burden to have a child and not be able to kill oneself proper. And promise me you won't eat that piece of bullshit like your momma asks. Okay. Promise me that. Don't have a kid, and don't take Communion."

There was no way Keagan could say no. He had to say yes. He gave a nod of his head so tiny he wasn't sure if his dad could see. He may have even said the word 'yes', maybe even crossed his heart and swore. Whichever way it was finally made clear, his dad was given a promise. Then Keagan walked off as if going to his bedroom but didn't go anywhere, just peered around the corner.

He heard his dad push three buttons on his cell phone, and after a short pause, his voice spoke stronger than he'd heard in months.

"The nature of my emergency is a man standing outside of his home with a gun. I'm looking at him now. There are kids around, too. No, nobody's hurt, not yet, but he's waving the gun and kids are about to be shot if you don't come fast. No, he's a white guy, scrubby beard, you better get there. Please, fast. He's at 15356 Ellen Drive."

The call ended. Keagan's dad reached for his prescription bottle, twisted the top off, and poured the contents into his throat. He took a dry gulp, pushed himself up with a moan, walked to the front door, and turned on the front porch light.

It was Halloween night, and the porch light was on.

That doesn't happen around here. *Halloween isn't for Christians. Not for real Christians. We don't hand out candy around here.*

Keagan's gut swirled. He put his hand over his mouth as if he might scream. He expected to hear the creak of his momma's bed and the thump of her feet coming down the hallway. But nothing.

Keagan quietly opened the front door and stepped outside to stand just behind his dad.

Children walked up the driveway like summertime bugs to the light. The first few looked at Keagan and he gave them a little wave, then put his hand back down before anyone saw his sin. His dad started handing out dollars, bending and straining with each move, his legs shaking.

A girl dressed as a clown, helium balloon in one hand, bag of candy in the other, got Dad's last dollar. That was when he heard the squeal of tires. Three cop cars had arrived from around the corner.

Keagan's dad dropped his wallet, pulled the gun from his back waistband, and took aim at the child.

Keagan's insides screamed.

His bowels loosened.

His chest tightened and was sure to explode if his dad shot the child.

Her mouth was stuck in a smile—a big, red-painted smile that covered her face—and she dropped the bag on the ground and let go of the balloon, which rose in the air.

Then came the gunshots. Not just one, but tons of them, snapping off like firecrackers. His dad's head jerked back, his shoulder wrenched backwards. It seemed he might fall but he held his ground, wobbled, and then aimed the gun towards the cops on the street. More shots were fired and each bullet sent chunks of his dad flying. He finally fell to the ground.

Then they shot him some more.

Keagan and the girl were wet with blood that had splattered from his dad's head as if a water balloon had burst. Body pieces were stuck on the window and stuck on the front door. The audience watching from the sidewalk were screaming. The police were yelling orders. Keagan stared down into his dad's face and saw the tiny slit of one of his eyes was still open. The other eye was blown apart and his head was caved in.

The clown girl cried and screamed.

Police barked more orders from the sidewalk.

Mayhem followed, with no order and nobody in charge.

In the middle of it, Keagan looked about the porch, picked at a piece of his dad that was stuck on his leg, opened up a Ziploc bag from his pocket, and stuck it inside.

It was all he could think to do.

Neighbors gathered in crowds. Ambulances came. Momma got up from bed but passed out, so the medics had to give her oxygen before taking Dad's body away.

Halloween night was spent talking to people in uniforms. Keagan finally went to bed at 2:47 in the morning and slept in his closet.

He woke after noon, not sure if it was a dream, not sure if the dark closet was real or outside of it was real. It was only when he felt in his pocket and squished the small piece of his dad's flesh in the Ziploc bag that he realized the truth.

His dad was dead.

He'd been shot right in front of him, and his soul had left his body from out of the bullet holes, to go wherever souls might go. All that Keagan had left was in his Ziploc, and he tucked it away in his closet.

He walked out of his bedroom to see people were gathered in his house. They looked at Keagan with suspicion, whispered to each other, and left soon after. Then his momma told him the plans.

"We have to bury him tomorrow on All Soul's Day, it's the only chance for the demon to be saved. It's the only way. Your daddy knew this, Keagan. That's what he wanted. That's why he died. And I think—now, I'm not sure—but I think he wanted you to die with him. A father should be with his son, it's why Jesus ascended to the right hand of his father."

Friends from church bought Keagan a proper suit to wear to the funeral, and they warned him he'd see his dad one last time. "Real Christians don't cremate, real Christians have an open casket."

Day of the funeral, Keagan knelt next to the casket, crossed himself the way everyone else did, and tried to recognize his father but couldn't. Part of his head was covered with a white cloth; the other was waxy plastic. This was some imposter lying there.

Church people visited the house afterwards, some driving from the church, even though it was faster to walk. They brought casseroles, mostaccioli, meatballs. They said what a troubled dad he had, (*but nobody deserved to die like that. God loves everyone, even saves wretched souls*). Keagan feigned agreement with everything he heard and made sure all of the adults in the house felt they were helping him.

Faith, the older girl from across the street, was the only one close to his age. Her hair was as black as her dress, as if made of the same silk. When she walked up to him and gazed into his eyes, his soul shrunk like a pupil in the bright light. She reached out and put a hand on his shoulder. He flinched, then melted.

She knows. She knows everything. She hears the words I do not say.

He wanted her to stop looking, to get her hand off him, to leave him alone and get out of his head. She muffled some words, gulped for air, and then started shaking. Weeping. Tears streamed down her face and her shaky hand moved to touch his cheek. Her skin was warm, clammy with sweat. Keagan felt the swirl of each fingerprint and watched her cry, jealous that he couldn't let his own insides ooze out the way she did.

"I saw. I watched it happen. And I heard. It was so loud," she said. Her eyes drifted off as if the memory of the bullets were tugging at her.

"That's enough, Faith," her dad said, and held forth a box of brownies for Keagan to take. "She lost her mom, too," he added as an explanation and then shuffled her off, somewhere beyond the room to where you take people who feel things the way she did.

The box of brownies were bought at the grocery store, nothing Faith's dad had made himself, and Keagan snuck off to put them into his closet. He placed them on the same shelf that held the snowman's heart and some old casserole, and the only piece of his dad that wasn't inside the casket. Keagan still couldn't tell what piece he'd collected, because part of it felt hard, like bone, and part of it felt fleshy, like the meat of his cheek.

Keagan spent the week with the sadness and hurt shredding him up inside. Sometimes it came out in the loneliness and quiet of the dark closet and he cried unseen, but mostly it stayed hidden in a part nobody could reach. Momma talked to him when she could, and told him more than once, "Your First Communion is coming soon, and then you'll be saved."

Promise me you won't eat that piece of bullshit like your momma asks.

The memories were tugging at him, too.

Chapter Three: Faith

The world never stopped screaming after Faith first produced life and felt it leak out of her body. It became the background noise to each breath, shrill as a morning ambulance siren, the kind that exploded her out of sleep, but these noises never faded down the street. They stayed inside her head and sliced up her eardrum, all from the bloody menstrual pad.

Instead of the garbage, Faith placed her used pads into a shoebox with care. Even though only one pad contained the monthly egg, she could not know which, so all of them were put into makeshift coffins. She used Nike boxes, Zappos boxes, Froot Loops boxes, whatever she could find to preserve the *beings,* because to discard any of them was discarding life. Like burying a miracle alive.

Like taking her mother off life support.

Faith tried to believe it made their suffering less, that without her tender care the shrieks would climb to such a howl it would crack the center of the earth and rip the mantle open, sucking down all living creatures into the fiery center. Living with the anguish was her penance for creating life. A small sacrifice to make.

She couldn't concentrate in school, and often had to close her eyes and rub her temples. They called her down to the principal's office and asked her if she was safe at home. Her father picked her up with assurances to the school that everything was fine, and then they drove home without a word to a silent dinner.

The screams kept her awake at night, and when she finally did sleep, it gave her nightmares of having a permanent ice cream headache with a frozen skull ready to crack. Other times she'd wake up in the middle of a dark night and the noise sounded like the soft hum of a humidifier.

Like my babies are sleeping.

She enjoyed those quieter moments and stared into the darkness until the night air seemed to swirl into shapes, tiny ghosts come to visit. But when the screams returned she could feel it at the base of her brain. Her bones would vibrate, like a tuning fork, and as the pitch screamed higher Faith ached to know what they wanted, what they needed. She was their creator, their only God, but she could not hear or understand their prayer. The eggs—there were ten by now—could only cry like an infant that could never be soothed.

When Faith was outside, the menstrual screams seemed to lift to the stars and come back down again, like the noise had air to breathe, and this gave her a slight reprieve.

It was like this on the Halloween night that ended in gunshots. The crunchy leaves released the smell of autumn into the air. The winter frost seemed it would never come. Candles burned behind the eyes of jack-o-lanterns. It was a perfect night.

Perfect until the gunshots.

Faith was handing out candy, once in a while eating a Kit-Kat and stuffing the wrapper in her pocket. As always on Halloween night, Keagan's house stayed dark, but when the porch did light up, kids were summoned to it.

Keagan's dad was there to greet them.

As if there was a police force on guard for this very moment, as if it were against the law for Keagan's house to end its reign of Halloween darkness, three squad cars pulled up.

Faith never saw Keagan's dad aim at the girl's head, she only saw the police men draw their own guns. She shut her eyes when the gunshots followed. Her heart split apart, and the cry of Faith's dying eggs went silent for the first time.

Faith opened her eyes and looked at the dead body in disbelief. Keagan looked back and then scrambled about the porch as if trying to put his dad back together.

When the ambulance finally came and took the body away, its siren was just another cry of terror into the night. It became clear that the fate of fertilized eggs who were born into this world and grew into adulthood were not much different than that of those abandoned.

Days later, Faith wore the black dress to the funeral and hoped it wouldn't add more darkness to the sad boy's life. His house needed some love, some cheer. Even though the family wasn't poor, they'd seemed so. She'd seen Keagan at church practicing walking up the aisle for the day he'd make his First Communion, hands folded in front of his body, but wearing the same shoes he'd been playing baseball in. It was like he had his dad's feet, but commanded forward by the might of his mom.

Every funeral Faith went to for the rest of her life would feel like her own mom's, and this one was no different. It was the scab of her mother's death ripped open, and seeing another child who lost a parent reminded her she would never heal. Faith could feel the adults whispering to each other, wondering what they should say to *the boy*. How will *the boy* handle it? They say *the boy* takes after his dad and maybe he was the one who made his dad go crazy and *lose it like that.*

Faith wanted to see Keagan, to show him he wasn't someone to be afraid of, so she approached him and put a hand on his shoulder. She gazed into his eyes and then lay a hand on his cheek. It felt like he'd been trembling from the same scream his whole life, as if the gunshots from the night of the shooting were still ricocheting around inside his hollowed-out body. This boy was alone, trapped, something vegetative inside him that maybe his Communion with Jesus might save. The brownies her dad brought wouldn't fill the space.

Faith went home, wondering if Keagan would find peace once his dad was in his final resting spot. She hoped it was under a beautiful, majestic tombstone that would guide Jesus to his body on judgment day. Faith could easily see her mom's tombstone when she closed her eyes, and the words etched into the granite: *If love alone could have saved you, you would have lived forever.*

Faith's own loved ones, her brood of life preserved in cardboard boxes, deserved their own glorious burial spot.

Chapter Four: Keagan's First Holy Communion

MORNING OF HIS COMMUNION, Momma said it was like her first child was getting married, only this one was getting married to Christ.

Keagan's heartbeat banged against his chest as he walked through the church parking lot. Everybody had on nicer black suits and shinier, tasseled shoes. His collar was so tight it pinched his neck, making it hard to swallow.

Inside the church, he genuflected in the aisle, same way he'd been taught to do, and sat in the pew. His stomach grumbled and he feared everybody would hear. He knelt when he was supposed to, shook hands and said "peace be with you" when he was supposed to, and crossed himself when he was supposed to. He wondered if his dad could see him wherever he was, and slipped his hand in his pocket.

If dad couldn't see him, at least he could be there. The Ziploc bag full of daddy parts was in his pocket, and Keagan squished it back and forth, all in private. Nobody knew, nobody could see.

Except.

He felt someone's eyes looking at him, right at the back of his head, like he'd been picked out. Found out. He turned to see.

It was Faith. Only this time the black locks of her hair were up in a bun instead of down on her shoulders, and the contrast against her white dress made her shine like an angel, a young angel, standing guard. She'd made her First Communion years ago, already lost a parent, already knew things. It seemed she knew what he was thinking and was waiting to see what he would do.

Keagan was waiting, too, not sure what to decide.

Promise me you won't eat that piece of bullshit like your momma asks.

Keagan was so hungry. He hadn't eaten breakfast since Momma said the body of Christ did not need to get tainted with Lucky Charms. He kept imagining the free pastries afterwards in the church basement. The outsides were stale and crusty, but sweet raspberry was in the middle. Soon enough, he would have the purple fruit dripping from his lips.

Finally, it came to the part where the priest hummed his hums and blessed the body and blood of Jesus. Keagan watched the people get in line, one line down the center to Father Richard, the other to the right, where the fake priest gave out the wafers.

Father Richard had them practice the walk he was about to make many times. How to fold their hands, walk in procession, and what to say when they got to the front of the line. Keagan imagined a hole opening up beneath him if he got it wrong, a flash of flame, and not even time for a screech before he got sucked down into Hell.

They walked in slow succession, like little men off to war. When they reached the front of the line, they craned their necks up at the priest who held the wafer in the air, like a dog trainer holding up a treat. "Body of Christ," he said, again and again, "Body of Christ." Each time someone new took a piece of Jesus on their tongue and then moved on.

"Body of Christ."

"Amen."

"Body of Christ."

"Amen."

And now it was Keagan's turn, the words he'd heard so many times were finally just for him. The eyes he looked up into were of God himself.

"Body of Christ."

As soon as Keagan mumbled, "Amen," the priest was in action. His thumb was strong, demanding, and planted the wafer on Keagan's tongue. Keagan's mouth watered and his gut swirled like a blender.

Promise me you won't eat that piece of bullshit like your momma asks.

What part of Jesus was in his mouth? Keagan kept wondering, but couldn't decide, since it felt like a piece of old, stale cardboard.

He returned to the pew, knelt down as he was taught, and put his hands in praying position. The wafer was soaking up his spit, sponging up his insides, and he knew he wasn't supposed to chew, so he didn't. He hunched his back, put his thumbs up against his lips, and with his tongue, pushed the piece of Jesus out of his mouth and into his hands.

Did anybody see?

He felt such fear in his gut he thought he'd puke. The wafer was moist between his fingers, and he waited for a tap on the shoulder from a man in uniform ready to pull him aside to a special room for committing such a sin. Or worse, he would burn, burn, burn in Hell as if locked inside an oven set it to broil.

But nothing. Nobody cared, so he just waited until it seemed he'd prayed long enough, cupped the wafer in his hand, and slipped it into his pocket. There was promise in the air when Mass finally ended, and the time came to leave. His tie felt a little less tight and the dark cloud in the room seemed to be leaving out the exits.

He traced his finger along the smooth top of the wooden pew walking to the aisle and there was Faith, standing in her white dress, her eyes tracking his every step. He could tell by the look in her eyes she'd been watching him, listening to his thoughts, like she herself was one of God's little helpers. Her knowing grin was either admiration or condemnation, Keagan couldn't tell which, but he walked right by and pretended not to notice.

But he did notice, and it felt like she was hovering over him even after he went home.

Once again his house was full of people from church. They told him how blessed he was to have Communion. Some gave him cards with dollar bills inside, and his mother took them to save before Keagan could return them to his closet. All the while he would poke his hand in his pocket, and feel the wadded up piece of wafer.

If they only knew the truth. He wasn't blessed.

After they'd all gone home and his momma had given him a goodnight kiss, he finally got back into his closet cavern. He turned on the flashlight and it felt like three a.m. with the soft hue of blue moonlight shining down. Finally, a chance to look at the wafer. It had dried up some, but was still pliable in his hands, like papier-mâché. He peeled the Jesus piece off his fingers and opened up the Ziploc with his dad's parts inside.

Dad's flesh had started to turn. Some spots were grey, others were purple, but since the wafer was gooey, he could wrap the piece of Jesus right around the gristle of his daddy's flesh.

See, Dad. I didn't swallow Jesus. Like I promised.

In the weeks that followed, the lights inside the house were usually off. Just Momma's bedside table lamp stayed on when Keagan brought her food. People from the church came. They wouldn't even knock on the door, just walked right in, since they knew Keagan's momma didn't get up except on Sundays when the Lord called her forth to Mass. They brought Keagan cookies and told him he needed to 'be good, for his mom's sake.'

"Tell your dad you love him," Momma would still remind Keagan like she always had.

"I can't Momma."

"Yes you can, you'll see him soon. You need to."

Months went by, and the church people stopped coming. Keagan worked hard to help his momma. He did things for her like changing the batteries on her remote so she could watch TV, and made his own dinners of peanut butter and jelly sandwiches. He spent the rest of his free time in his closet. The dark inside was his friend and it missed him when he was gone. Both of them were empty without each other.

Some days he didn't go to school, and Momma didn't know. He woke in the morning from his closet to find it was too late, his Momma still asleep, and he'd hide there until school was over. School was getting worse since stories of the upcoming Halloween night were spreading. Older boys whispered dares to each other about who would trick-or-treat at his house. Some would make pistols out of their fingers and fire at Keagan's head in the hallway.

Boom-Boom.

He had nothing to fire back with.

Only thing that was missing from his closet, only thing he wish he had, was his dad's gun. The police returned the gun after the investigation and Momma hid the box somewhere in the house. Keagan had searched for it, but only found the bullets in her bedside drawer as she slept; no gun to be found. Momma hardly left her room, so it was hard to search any deeper to find the pistol.

Sundays were the only day Momma ever seemed to move. She'd have to fight to get out of bed, and the bed creaked loudly like it needed oiling, and she'd say things like, "You've cursed me. The weight is too much. We need to lift it. Your dad did it right. You're next."

Mom wouldn't go to Communion. She said she didn't need to, but she'd watch Keagan each time, and when Keagan heard Father Rick say, "Body of Christ," he always heard the voice of his dad right afterwards: *Promise me you won't eat that piece of bullshit like your momma asks.*

After taking the Body of Christ on his tongue, Keagan would push the wafer to the roof of his mouth, kneel down to pray in the pew, spit the wafer out into his hands, and then slip the wafer into his pocket. Nobody saw a thing.

Each Sunday, he'd bring the piece home, and over the weeks, the mass of wafers grew bigger, big as a football. Soon enough, he shaped it into a tiny figure with little legs, arms and a round head.

Life inside the closet was changing.

The worm in the Ziploc bag had started to wiggle again, and the black ants started to crawl all over it, eating the worm alive like they were before. The bag full of water was back to being a frozen snowball again, just waiting to get transplanted back into a snowman's chest. Keagan took it out of the bag and it froze his fingers so badly he had to put it back.

And the tiny little guy he made from chunks of Jesus flesh sat across from him while he played games like Stratego, Battleship, and Connect Four. Each week, the new Communion wafer gave it longer arms, legs, and a tiny bump for a nose. Keagan used his fingernails to carve out eyes and a mouth.

At night, Keagan sometimes felt he could hear the ghost of his dad taking his late night walks down the hallway, groaning in pain, looking for his prescription bottle. During the day, he sometimes saw the Lazy-Boy rocking, and he'd turn the TV to SportsCenter, just in case.

His dad's collection of Louisville sluggers, made of ash, series 5 and 7, with cursive signatures, seemed confused about his dad's absence, as if they were his pets, wondering where their master had gone. When Keagan held them he felt powerful. He wished his dad could lob him a pitch all the way from his grave.

He carried a bat onto the porch, the last place his dad was alive, and tapped it on the ground, using it like a cane. He gazed across the way at the church and wondered if he should genuflect when the church gazed back.

But more than the church, it was the tiny white gravestones in front of St. Mary's that seemed to speak to him. Just white whispers muttered in the wind. The rows of white crosses were called *The Cemetery of the Innocents,* and were there to honor aborted children. Momma had explained that he could have been aborted, too, and one of those crosses would be just for him.

Something seemed wrong.

The perfectly uniformed rows of crosses seemed to have been mowed down. Some of them were tilted out of the ground, like a tiny tornado had spun through, leaving a path of them wrecked. The crosses that remained stood guard with extra vigilance.

And as happened so often, he saw Faith tending to *The Cemetery of the Innocents*, mysteriously burying into the earth, and then scurrying about like an ant whose home had been stepped upon.

Keagan walked over, slowly, banging the bat on the ground with each step, acting like he wasn't really interested. He crossed the street, and got a closer look at the wooden crosses that had been snapped in half. The jagged edges that stuck out towards the sky were no longer crosses, but sharp spears, stabbing at the heavens. The damaged bits of splintered wood rested on the ground.

Before Faith could see, Keagan reached down to a broken piece and peeled back a sliver of wood from the cross. He planned to place it in his closet, right on top of the daddy bits wrapped in wafers.

Chapter Five: Faith at the Cemetery

FAITH PICKED UP the broken pieces, straightened the leaning crosses, and then knelt in front of the last damaged grave marker as if paying homage. The grass hadn't yet dried from the day's watering and her pants were getting wet, but the moist ground was easy to dig. She used her fingernails as a shovel, first by stabbing them into the earth, then lifting out a sod of grass and making a six-inch deep hole. She looked to both sides with suspicion, waiting to see if anyone was watching. *Nobody will see*, she told herself, *you're invisible*, so she pulled the menstrual pad, still wet with life-fluid, from her pocket. She placed it in the shallow grave, said a silent prayer, and then covered it with dirt.

The burial ceremony was over.

She'd been coming to *The Cemetery of the Innocents* each month while having her period to give her discarded life-blood a proper burial and a sacred resting place. During those last moments, just before she placed the remains in the earth, the screams shot up into the sky as if the tiny creatures were being cremated alive. But soon as she lowered them in the ground, the noise faded like a crying baby succumbing to sleep.

The quiet that followed confirmed to her she was doing the right thing. Burying her discarded eggs, placing them in the ground, and waiting for the Second Coming. Salvation was possible. The cross that marked their grave was proof of this. The earth was a warm, natural blanket for their final resting spot.

Faith still had the soft dirt in her hands when she felt a bolt of fear. Someone was close by. She felt a change in the weather.

She glanced over her shoulder and saw Keagan standing there holding a bat. His pants were stained and his shirt hung over his skinny body like his whole stomach and chest cavity had caved in. He wanted her attention, she could tell, and even though she felt all the sadness of his heart inside her own, she wished he hadn't come here. He was an intruder in these parts. A man. A bat. Both of these ripe with violence.

"What happened?" he finally asked.

"Oh, nothing. Just murder. Children killed before they were born," Faith answered. She ran her hand over the grass and imagined the green blades were bangs of hair growing from underneath. If others knew there was indeed something buried here, maybe they'd pay the graves more respect and not vandalize them.

"I mean how did they break?" he asked, a lot louder than he needed to.

"The swift kick from a bitter vandal. People don't want to face the daily holocaust of abortion. Every day, children are siphoned out of pregnant women and left in medical dispensers and then burnt in waste dumps. Each of these grave sites represents a dead fetus. Life's too precious. Protect life."

Life. The sound hung in the air, and then her silence was the exclamation point.

"Shouldn't these be urns, then? Since the dead fetuses will be burned to ash."

"Cenotaphs, graves without bodies," Faith said, and then muttered, "most of them," not even sure if he heard, but quite certain he didn't know what *cenotaphs* meant (she'd only just learned herself). But it didn't matter. He wasn't leaving as she hoped, but kept putting the bat over his shoulder, like a batter ready to swing, waiting for a pitch.

"What are you doing with that bat?"

"It's my dad's," he said, as if that was an answer. "I'm just going to hit some rocks. It's fun, you should try it."

Faith knew her time was lost here, the peace shattered by this younger boy, so she stood up, wiped the dirt off her legs, and agreed. "Okay, let's hit some rocks."

On the other side of the church from *The Cemetery of the Innocents*, past the parking lot, was a mini basketball court, half the size of a real court, with lowered hoops and rainbow-nets. Farther back was a baseball backstop in front of a rocky infield. Faith had seen Keagan with his dad there before, but not hitting rocks—hitting tennis balls. This was the only time Keagan's dad came close to St. Mary's church.

Keagan shuffled his feet through the rocky dirt and went straight for the batter's box. Faith went to the pitcher's area.

"How do you do this?"

"You just grab a stone and throw so I can hit it. You see the rocks all over. Pick them up and toss."

Faith reached down, grabbed a handful of rocks, and siphoned through them as if sifting for gold. Keagan held the bat over his head. The first rock she tossed was a tiny one, and it veered in the wind and smashed into his side. By the sound of it, right into a rib.

"Ouch," he squeaked in pain, trying to hold back tears,

"Sorry!" she yelled. "Not used to throwing these. Not used to throwing."

Keagan pulled up his shirt and a red welt was already on the side. He stared at the welt as if expecting it to do something.

"I can't throw like your dad," Faith added, trying to sound warm and understanding, but realizing it sounded cold.

She grabbed a bigger rock and lobbed it over the plate. It was a perfect pitch that curved right into the strike zone. He laid down the lumber, kept his head down, spun his waist, pushed off on his back foot, all like his dad taught him, and he smashed the rock in the air. They both craned their necks looking up. They lost it in the sun, eyes squinted, waiting until it rained down and they both heard it land.

"Good one," she said. He crouched down again, eager for the next pitch. She threw another. He smashed this one, too, and cocked the bat over his shoulder ready for another. She lobbed one too high, and he swung and missed. She threw another, this time faster, and it whizzed near his ear.

"You're trying to hurt me, aren't you?'

She realized she could hurt him by doing this. One stone might hit his temple and knock out his brain. Make him vegetative. *No sign of brain waves.*

Faith put her arms to her side, relaxed her fingers, and let the remaining rocks fall to the ground. Keagan took the bat off his shoulder.

"You want me to pitch?" he said, and picked up a handful of stones before she could answer. He handed Faith the bat. She hadn't swung one since 5th grade softball, and even then she just felt awkward.

"You know, the Bible thinks people should be stoned for their sins," Faith said. "Makes me wonder if we're all here just to stone each other. All of us each other's devils."

"Well, I'm sure you have never sinned, so you're fine."

Keagan started to wind up for his first pitch, arms bobbing up and down, but before he could throw Faith interrupted.

"You miss your dad. I know it. But you'll see him again. You will."

Keagan lost himself. His whole body turned to the side in the middle of his wind-up, and he chucked a rock high into the air towards the church where a group of people were walking to their car. Faith and Keagan held their breath as they watched it arc, like a rainbow, waiting to see if it would hit any of the churchgoers. Faith wanted to cry out, tell them to move away, but it wouldn't do any good. All she could do was say a quick prayer.

The rock finally came back down, harmlessly well past the group, and smashed into tinier bits. The group was unhurt and unaware. Faith felt Keagan's relief.

"Do they stone people for suicide?" Keagan asked while he looked for the next rock to pitch. "Suicide is a sin, right?"

"You think your dad killed himself?"

"Maybe. What's it matter? He's dead."

"It matters. It matters a lot. Some people think if you kill yourself you won't go to Heaven. That changes if you'll see him again or not."

Keagan pitched a stone, Faith took a swing and fouled it off behind her. She could sense Keagan thinking, deciding if he should say more, and she let him think without interrupting.

"It was suicide by cop," Keagan finally said. "He called the police and pulled out his gun on purpose."

Keagan seemed defeated by his confession and shuffled his feet on the ground.

"It's okay. Really," Faith assured him. "Jesus did the same. He knew he was going to be betrayed and killed, but walked right into it. Your dad was no different. He didn't pull the trigger, someone else did."

Keagan grunted, because he agreed with her or was angry with her, she couldn't tell which.

"What about your mom?" he asked. "She didn't know she was going to die, right?"

Faith didn't answer, and wouldn't, but it made her think. *My mom was about to be killed and was begging for help, but I didn't stop it.*

"And what have you been burying under those crosses?"

Keagan's words smacked her like a stone to the forehead, but hurt so much worse. *He knows? How can he know?* She was suddenly scared, violated, like she'd been spied on. Like her children weren't safe.

Faith gripped the bat tightly, squeezing as if trying to break the wood, and then dropped it on the ground.

"You'll see your dad again, Keagan. Don't worry. Someday, when Jesus walks the earth, the dead will rise and all souls will be judged. Your dad had a good soul. I know it. Until then, you'll just have to wait."

Faith turned for home, leaving Keagan by himself.

As she walked home past the white crosses, she realized she was no longer invisible. The boy across the street *saw* her, everyone *saw* her—what happens in the dark comes to light.

She decided it was time to stop hiding. She found a cross that she knew was empty and straddled it from above, one leg on each side. She unbuttoned the top of her pants and reached her hand down. Her skin was wet and clammy from anger, from fear, from the boy who knew things, but she didn't care. She kept reaching down her pants. She knew someone might think she was sinning right then and there, but they would be wrong.

She pulled out the pad with one hand, ripped up a piece of earth with the other, and buried the pad in the hole. Another one to add to the cemetery. If all these eggs in the ground needed to be fed, she'd surely not have enough, but if Jesus came, nourishment would be bountiful.

She went home and cried in bed, knees pulled up to her chest, arms wrapped around her legs, gently rocking. Her tears finally stopped when sleep came.

She began to dream and her spirit lifted from her body, floated above her bed, and she looked down at herself sleeping. The hair on one side of her head had been shaven, revealing a sliced-open skull. Tubes came out of her and were attached to medical equipment. Her dad came into her bedroom, ripped the tubes out, while Faith prayed to Jesus to make him stop.

Chapter Six: Keagan

KEAGAN WATCHED FAITH leave the baseball field and waited until she disappeared out of sight. Then he bent down to grab the biggest rock within arm's reach, tossed it straight up, and quickly cocked the bat over his shoulder. He swung and hit the rock with a savage howl. The stone went sailing like a rocket straight at the church. Keagan watched, waited, praying that it would hit some stained glass. The shattering crash would change things forever.

He held his breath, his heart beat faster, his eyes opened wider. Any second and the church would be shattered.

The rock landed against the brick, between two windows, and blew apart like pieces of dust.

Missed again.

Nothing changed.

Keagan tapped the bat on the ground and walked, past the backstop, past the mini basketball court, and to *The Cemetery of the Innocents*. The crosses stood like trees in a forest that held secrets they'd never reveal.

But Keagan did know one of their secrets.

He walked to a cross in the middle of the bunch and started to claw at the earth, same way he'd seen Faith do, and it wasn't long until he found something buried. This cross was no *cenotaph*.

Whatever it was, it was wrapped up inside paper towel and covered with dirt. He put it inside a Ziploc bag from his front pocket, and took it home.

In the safety of his bedroom he opened up the Ziploc and unraveled the mysterious gift. It took a moment for him to understand where he recognized the scent from, where he'd seen something like this before, but then he remembered. It was from the forbidden parts of his momma's garbage can. *A feminine napkin*. Something about women that boys didn't need. Parts boys weren't supposed to know about, and certainly weren't supposed to dig up.

Why would Faith bury this? It was something special to her, something pulled from deep in her heart, so dear that she buried it in a special grave. Just like her mom was buried, and just like his dad. He thought about going back to the cemetery and putting it back where she wanted it. She was the only kind face he'd seen in so long. Even if she did stomp off with a huff, she'd taken the time to play with him, talk to him, and explain things.

With all of that, wouldn't he want a part of her with him always?

He packaged it up in the Ziploc bag and put it on the closet shelf, with the sliver of wood from the broken cross to mark its spot.

Chapter Seven: Keagan

BY THE ANNIVERSARY of his dad's death, the sadness that had grown dry threatened to erupt from Keagan's eyes. It rumbled beneath the surface ready to explode. He couldn't stop thinking about last year.   His dad asking him to fetch the box from the closet. The little girl's fright when his dad took aim. The snap of gunfire from the police. The look on his dad's mangled face as he lay dead on the porch. All of it a fresh vision in his mind's-eye.

Keagan wished he could be somebody else on this Halloween night, wished he could dress up as a monster or a hero, anything but the boy who lived at the house everyone feared. No way would Momma let him wear a costume. He didn't even ask.

Halloween was on a Monday. Keagan couldn't escape going to school, but after school let out and the sun went down, he rushed home, planning to stay in his closet all night and pretend the world didn't exist. He hopped up the steps of his front porch, (still stained with blood from a year ago) ran inside, locked the front door, and pulled the shades. He thought about somehow escaping his house, or no, escaping his body, but he was trapped inside both of them.

Momma's light was on in the hallway, but it seemed like the wind was blowing it on and off, on and off. Keagan got closer, and he saw why.

A candle was lit bedside, the firelight highlighting her face. Her face changed colors with the flame, shades of orange on her cheek glowing, and her eyes open wide, not blinking. She sat on the edge of her bed, legs leaning over, as if she was uncertain whether to get up or lie back down.

A gun sat on her lap. His dad's gun, nestled like a black kitten. She didn't look up at Keagan when she started to speak.

"You were supposed to go with him, Keagan, don't you see? And you have to go tonight."

"Where? Where am I going, Momma?"

"To see your dad. You understand why. I know you do. Come here and give me a hug first."

His heart was punctured, and from the wound, tears finally broke free. Warm tears, hot as blood, streamed down his cheeks. He stepped forward.

Momma held out her chubby claw of an arm and she rolled Keagan up inside. With her other hand, she picked up the gun and pressed it against his head.

The pistol was cold, pure, menacing. It wanted to be fired. Keagan could tell that the cold tip of the metal gun wanted to splatter his brains. He waited to hear the click of the trigger and feel the bullet shatter his skull.

"I love you, my sinner."

Click.

She gasped, pulled again, ***Click,*** and again, ***Click,*** each click quicker than the last, each time he winced but didn't die. He was still breathing, his heart still beating, his brain still thinking, face sweating from being wrapped up in her chubby arms.

"I need to load it. Stay here," she said, and released him.

Keagan didn't stay there but stumbled to the bedroom door. He turned to see his momma fumbling through the drawer on her bedside table. Maybe he should have just stayed there, let her kill him, and die to make her happy.

Don't swallow the bullshit your momma's wanting to feed you.

He fought off the urge to obey and took off down the hall, shut his bedroom door behind him, and went straight to his closet to hide in the darkness.

Keagan wanted to be the worm in the bag, squirming around his closet. He wanted to be a potato chip crumb, something so tiny his momma couldn't see him. He pulled his legs up into his chest, made himself into a little ball, and rocked back and forth.

Time passed, time didn't count. He was alone, and waiting for the closet door to open and his mother to shoot. He imagined the feel of the bullet poking through his skull, into his brain, feeling it explode. He just wished it was over. If he had the gun, he'd do the deed and just kill himself.

Some people think if you kill yourself you won't go to Heaven. That changes if you'll see him again or not.

His dad wasn't here to protect him anymore, all he had was the dark blanket of his closet to hide in, so he sat alone waiting to be killed. But before that could happen, the dark of the closet started to come alive. He could hear it breathing, feel it in motion. The warm cloud of sour breath filled the air. A hand grabbed his shoulder, and he felt an explosion inside.

A flash of brilliant white light. More brilliant than the darkness had ever been, like the blood in his veins was made of lightning. The incredible pain he feared from the gunshot never came—instead the emptiness he'd had since birth was gone. Zapped out of him. A warmness so pleasant took its place, like a campfire on a cold night that warms your cheeks and makes them glow. It built with such joy he wanted to sing. Or maybe he was singing, because he heard music in the air.

It wasn't Momma with a gun who had put her hands on him, but a man. Keagan stared into his eyes, expecting him to cry, begging him to, since his eyes seemed stuck on the edge of tears that wouldn't spill over. They stayed there, frozen in sadness. The sadness got deeper, grew like a root into Keagan's back, and soaked up his years of hurt and disappointment.

Keagan reached out to touch him, and brushed a finger along his cheek.

His flesh was a dried up Communion wafer. His body was held together by Keagan's saliva over the last year. Somewhere underneath it all was a chunk of his dad. This was the *Body of Christ*, brought to life.

Christ scooped Keagan into his arms, and held him like a tiny babe. Keagan could have stayed there forever but instead the Lord carried Keagan to the hallway, set him on the ground, and took him by the hand. Keagan felt the puncture wounds on Christ's palm, and could see the gaping wounds on his bare feet. A ring of cuts circled around his forehead, and a wound on his side oozed a bit with each step he took. Father Richard had explained Jesus was given one last stab to make sure he was dead, and it made Keagan think of vampires that needed a stake through the heart to kill them.

But this was no vampire, this was his Savior.

Keagan wondered if he was already dead, if his momma had already shot him, and now he was just being carried by Jesus, to either Heaven or Hell, where he hoped he would see his dad. They walked to the front door. Jesus flicked on the porch light, and stepped outside into the light.

Their house was open on Halloween.

Keagan's stomach boiled with excitement. He felt like a jack-o'-lantern himself, smugly tucked into his Maker's arms, for the light inside made his eyes glow.

The sidewalk was full of trick-or-treaters, and as soon as Jesus carried Keagan onto the porch, he could feel heads turn, jaws drop, faces cringe. Swarms of kids walked the sidewalks, bundled in the crisp autumn air. None of them wanted to visit the house that should forever stay dark on Halloween night, even after the porch became lit by the light of Christ.

Instead, they stood on the sidewalk, watched, and waited. If last year's bloody death didn't scare them away, then this Jesus, this golem made of Communion wafers and bits of his dad's flesh, certainly did. But finally a girl, guided by parents unaware of what had happened a year before, walked up the driveway. She had to raise her knees high to get up the porch steps, and then she held open a pillowcase without saying a word. Keagan wanted her to come closer, to feel the glow of Jesus.

Tell all of them, tell everyone, spread the word, there's nothing to fear in this house tonight.

He waited to see what Jesus would do with no candy to give.

And then he heard those familiar words.

"Body of Christ."

Keagan expected her to run, but she did not. She stood transfixed, her muscles relaxed, her soul in a spell. She tilted her head in confusion and Keagan tried to figure out her costume. Her face was made up in some anime character he had never seen.

"Body of Christ," Jesus said again, and this time Christ raised his hand to the side of his neck, tore at his skin, and clawed out a bit of his flesh as if peeling off a scab. He held it forth between his fingers.

"Body of Christ," Jesus said again.

"Amen," the cartoon girl responded. She opened her mouth, presented her tongue, and Jesus placed the scabby piece of his own flesh on top.

Her face contracted. Her tongue swooshed about her mouth. Her eyes lit up. Her face didn't smile as much as show relief, every muscle melting in comfort, the ending of some long suffering found. She walked down the porch to her parents a different girl than the one they knew. Glowing like a firefly in the darkest of nights.

A steady march happened shortly after. Kids of all heights and ages lined up in single file. All of them in costume and staring up at the man full of spike wounds on his hands and a bloody ring around his head. His body looked like chewed up crackers and bits of ham, and the children who were looking for candy instead received a piece of Jesus on their tongue. *Amens* came out of their mouths from a place deep within their soul.

"Body of Christ."

"Amen."

And a ninja gets a meaty piece from Jesus's cheek.

"Body of Christ."

"Amen."

And Captain America gets a piece from Jesus's palm.

"Body of Christ."

"Amen."

And a zombie gets a piece of Jesus's forehead.

This wasn't Halloween anymore, this night when the dead were allowed to walk the earth; it was something more. Something holy, and the neighborhood felt it more than knew it, for they were coming faster with each moment. Jesus pulled chunks off himself as if there was an endless, bountiful supply, and each child swallowed the gift and left in a halo of joy. Keagan stood solemnly alongside, making eye contact with each customer, and wished he had some wine.

All his life had led to this moment.

A creak behind him shattered it apart.

The front door opened. Momma stood behind him, filling up the doorway. Her hair was a matted mess. Her eyes burned with rage.

"Get away from that thing, Keagan."

Keagan stood still. Jesus turned to face her. His momma's fat cheeks turned red with fury.

"Keagan. Repent. Repent now, or I shall deliver you to Hell."

Keagan felt the warm flame inside him blow out, and his chest filled with dark smoke. His momma's hair seemed to grow, each strand a hissing snake, the gun in her hand the cobra ready to strike. Jesus stood before her with arms outstretched, the way he'd seen him stand in bookmarks and posters.

"To Hell with you," she said.

The gun fired.

Keagan hadn't screamed the night his dad died, but at that moment he screamed in horror, his mouth wide open, and the pain of all history poured forth from a bottomless cavern deep in his gut. Jesus was blown apart. Bits of his blood splattered on the front window, chunks of flesh on Keagan's face, and a pool of bloody wine puddled on the porch where Jesus now lay.

"You too, Keagan. You too."

Keagan waited for the shot his momma had been wanting to take since the day he was born. He wanted to die, wanted to join his dad and Jesus and let his blood mix with both of theirs on the front porch.

"All right then, I'll go to Hell," Keagan said in defiance. His momma took aim. Her body shook, her hand unsteady, but before she could shoot, her eyes lost focus, and she looked at Jesus.

He was moving.

The crumbled mess of blood and Communion wafers on the porch had started to move. His legs pulled him back upright, a waterfall of blood poured from the wound on his side, but he stood before them.

The miracle filled Keagan's soul with joy, and the Lord reached out a finger and touched his face. A piece of Jesus's own flesh had stuck to his cheek, and Christ took it off and then held it forth to Keagan's mom.

"Body of Christ."

Her body went slack, like her spine had been lifted right out of her.

"Amen. Amen…" she repeated until she could speak no more and her mouth hung open.

Jesus placed the bloody piece of flesh on her wet tongue. She took it eagerly, like a starving dog getting fed. She squished it about her mouth, her cheeks chomped away, and then she forced a swallow.

Keagan waited. Jesus did, too.

Soon enough she dropped her gun and started to gag. She gasped for air, sucking in each breath harder than the last. Her hands wrapped around her neck. Her tongue waggled out between her teeth, and then turned black as if roasted.

She fell to the ground with a crackling scream. A Halloween witch burning at the stake.

Keagan waited to feel sad. Nothing came.

Then Jesus spoke. "Body of Christ," he said.

Keagan didn't remember saying, "Amen," but he felt it, and he had no doubt that this was a real piece of Jesus-flesh ready to go into his mouth. After the bloody piece was placed on his tongue, he gulped it down whole, and the Eucharist tasted nothing like fake wafers from church, but rather like the smoke from the factory Dad worked in years ago. Keagan was now part of Jesus forever, in full Communion with the Lord. But he'd broken his promise to his dad.

But it wouldn't be the first broken promise.

For soon after swallowing the piece of Jesus's flesh, he saw a tiny creature crawling slowly on the ground just inside the front door. At first he thought it was a giant bug, then he realized it was human. It had a face—little bug eyes that were not yet open, and its skin was bloody. It was dragging its body towards him, like an infant to its daddy.

He could see the tiny infant looked just like Faith, and was drenched in the blood from her feminine napkin.

Chapter Eight: Faith

HALLOWEEN NIGHT AT DUSK.

Her dad had filled a bowlful of Reese's Peanut Butter Cups and set it on the kitchen table. Next to the candy lay the white Phantom of the Opera mask. Faith saw the Phantom when she was nine and came home with the program, a T-shirt, and the plastic white mask. Faith wanted to be Christine, and her mom the phantom. The last Halloween her mom was alive she had worn the mask all night long. Faith could still see the smile on her face, half of it mysteriously hidden by the white plastic, the other half full of joy.

Faith took the bowl of candy outside and sat on the front porch. The night was calm, waiting for the trick-or-treaters to slice through the silence. Soon the front doors would open and she'd hear the chatter of excited youth, but for now the neighborhood was a smooth pond without a ripple.

Her life had become a smooth pond as well.

The constant cries for help that used to fill her ears and saturate her soul were gone, except for those few days a month when she had her period. The noise started with a small tickle in her ear and then moved into a squeal. The more she bled, the higher the pitch. Every few hours she would wrap up the sticky red pad as if it were a precious jewel, and then walk the remains to their burial spot.

The Cemetery of the Innocents stood watch across the street to one side of her house, while straight across the street, Keagan's front porch was dark. He was surely inside, and she figured if he ever heard a scream reach out from his memory, it would be on this night—the anniversary of his dad's death. Memories can do that, and every single molecule on this street, every bit of oxygen, every blade of grass, remembered what happened exactly one year before.

Faith tapped her feet waiting for someone to come by. No trick-or-treaters yet, so she sat alone. "I'll be inside if you need me," Faith's dad had said, which surely meant he'd be on his computer listening to music. Even if her dad was with her, neither of them would speak. It was like they'd both become deaf and neither of them could sign and were forbidden to learn. Faith found herself wishing her period would come. At least then she knew she was alive and had a purpose, even if the experience was suffering.

Halloween night was when the dead were supposed to walk the earth, but that was foolish, for she knew it was only Jesus who would come to Judge the living and the dead.

But what if...

What if her mom could return to life? She would have questions, she would be angry, vengeful, even, at those who let her die when she could have been kept alive. Now she'd been forgotten. Faith couldn't remember the last time she heard her dad say Mom's name.

Faith took a deep breath of the autumn air, and then decided to leave the bowl on the porch and abandon her post. She thought about writing a note: "Take Just One Please," but whoever would follow those rules didn't need to be told, and whoever would break them would break them anyways.

She opened her front door with a slow twist and went inside, making sure to guide the screen door closed to avoid the metallic *clank*. She went into the bathroom, turned on the light, then leaned into the mirror. She stared into her own eyes and stopped her eyelids from blinking until focus went in and out. Her vision changed, reality twisted, and she reached for her dad's razor. She started shaving through the thick hair on one side of her head. It came out in clumps and she had to whack at it like using a machete through a rainforest. Soon the sink was full of locks of hair and one side of her head was shaven.

She held the razor on edge and cut a line of skin on her shaven scalp. A stinging pain shot down her spine and blood drip,

drip, dripped into the sink. A few pats with toilet paper stopped the flow enough, and she walked out of the bathroom with just a small trickle of blood down the side of her head. The cut didn't need the stitching up her mom's did, but looked just as bloody.

The phantom mask looked up at her from the kitchen table. The mask was empty, the eye socket black. They needed each other.

She put the mask over her own face. It fit nicely, and quickly became a part of her. She was full phantom, and her new face helped her walk those next few steps to the kitchen. She pulled the largest of the steak knives out of the wooden block and gripped the plastic handle tightly in her hand. She twisted the metal side to side. It was long enough to *pull the plug*. Revenge fantasies wormed in and out of the cracks in her head and she walked trance-like down the hall.

She pushed the bedroom door open. His face was to the wall at his desk, his ears wrapped up in his headphones, and she crept towards him, knife in front leading the way. Soon she was within reach. She held the knife at the base of his neck.

She sliced his neck across the jugular, she stabbed his side again and again, she cut through his skull until his brains came out, she imagined killing her dad a thousand ways in that instant, wondering which one was best, waiting for something; for him to cry out, for her mom to come back, for the screams to comfort her again, to finally be noticed. She wanted to hear her dad beg to be kept alive, same way she heard her mom's voice the night she died. Then he might finally understand.

Finally, he turned, spotted her, and jumped up from his chair. Their eyes made communion, locked in to each other, and she felt a history of loss and hurt and loneliness and emptiness get sucked out of her.

For that moment, she didn't just look like her mom, but had become her mom, and that's what he saw. He had finally looked into the eyes of the woman he had killed. She didn't thrust the knife—she didn't need to.

The dead had walked into his life. He deserved to be haunted.

Faith ripped the mask from her face, dashed out of the bedroom, down the hallway, and out the front door of her house. The screen door slammed with a metallic *clank,* and she made quick strides across the street.

She was off to the life amongst the crosses, those who were just as lonely as she was. She wanted to feel the presence of the eggs she'd made in her womb, those who were left to die, same as her own mother, same as her own motherhood.

She walked through the row of white crosses. They were soldiers to march for her, to fight whatever war she wished. She sat on the ground among them, cross-legged, and then stretched out to lay flat on the earth. The grass contoured around her body, cradling her like a babe. She imagined she could hear the heartbeat of Mother Earth below, deep under the mantle.

The knife was still in one hand, and with each lonely moment, she realized she could kill herself with it and then be sucked right down into Hell below, but decided to bear the loneliness. Another victory fought and won alone.

The stars twinkled like Christmas lights above her, and she wished she could hear them as well. She imagined they were looking at her, blinking in silent Morse codes, trying to speak. The many colors were just the many eyes of God, protecting her, ready to embrace her and never let her go.

She heard the creak of a front door opening, and before she even looked knew whose door it was—it was Keagan's. She craned her neck and saw a figure step out onto his front porch. The person was full of vibrant light. It was as if the stars above had found themselves a place in the tall man's chest. Next to him stood Keagan, the fatherless boy.

Something inside Faith quaked. The grumble of faraway thunder seemed to come from inside her own chest. The ground itself started to shake. She held out her hands for balance, but then everything was shattered by gun fire.

The snap of the gunshots echoed from the heavens. The figure on Keagan's porch had been shot and fell to the ground. It was last year all over again. Her vision, her spirit, her gaze all grew unsteady.

What was happening?

As if to answer, the ground under her clearly started shifting, and the crosses started to shake. First one, then another, then too many to count, as if a gopher was burrowing in the ground and knocking them loose.

She felt the pinch of a bug on her ankle, sharp as a bee sting, and bent forward to itch but stopped.

It was no bug. It was no autumn mosquito living longer than it should, but two tiny fingers reaching out of the grass, pinching her skin.

She watched as a hand came out of the ground, twisting and clutching, grasping, and pulling. The flesh was white against the dark earth, brought to life as if Jesus himself had come to raise the dead. Faith's mouth hung open in shock but her lungs were too scared to breathe.

The full arm reached out from the grave, tiny and frail, followed by little shoulders. It's little arms frantically clawed to escape from its tomb, until finally, the head emerged.

It seemed to Faith like a tadpole version of a human, not fully formed, not ready to walk, but needing to *eat*. Its tiny, fish-like mouth puckered, as if sucking at a nipple that could not be found.

All around her more of the creatures were sprouting out of the ground, their tiny fingers reaching out of the soil, grasping at the earth, pulling themselves up with scrawny arms. Their faces emerged from the ground, little bug eyes not fully open, mouths sucking at the air. The beings were bloody, same as a newborn, and just as hungry, for each suck of oxygen was followed by a wailing cry to the heavens. It was a cry she knew well, for she had heard it the first day of every menses. The cries that cut into her eardrums and made her eyes water with tears of glass, were back.

And together the sounds fused into one voice, and made words.

Blood.

Bread.

Blood and bread.

Blood and bread.

Unable to walk but furiously desperate, they had to use their arms to drag their bodies. Reach, drag, reach, drag, a full dozen of them now crawling towards Faith who lay in the middle. She was full of love and full of fear, watching them come to life, wondering how she could feed them all.

And when their tiny eyes opened like flowers slowly blooming, each eyelid a golden ray of sun, she saw her mother's eyes.

The faces were like her own—not fully developed, still wet and glimmering with blood—but not the eyes.

When they opened, Faith was looking into the eyes of her own mother, as she had prayed would happen at the hospital. Jesus answers prayers, always right on time.

Faith created the infants, and their frantic demand for **Blood and Bread** would have to be satisfied. The hungry newborns crawled towards her through the grass, their albino flesh glistening from menstrual blood, each of them moving towards their mother. They were sexless, hairless, each one looking up to her with the affection of a puppy. Their nostrils not yet fully formed, their useless feet and legs had to be dragged behind, their tiny arms and tiny digits with translucent skin, and just below the flesh she could see the tiny veins pumping with life.

And then the bites came. Their teeth had not yet formed but they chomped down with their gums. It felt to Faith like the pinch of a garter snake, and any urge to flinch was stopped by the glorious song from her own heart that these were her children, come to their mother.

Blood and Bread. They were starving, these innocents, but with each suckle they grew more dissatisfied, and screeched with pain. The sound of their wailing made her soul grow cold. If she had a bit of mercy in her heart she would put these tiny creatures to death and end their suffering. All she had to do was grab the knife and slice their necks, pull the plug on their life, and stop the torture of their existence.

Instead, she gripped the knife in one hand, held out her other hand, and sliced the flesh of her palm. It stung, like a deep paper cut, and after a short pause blood streamed down the lined cut. She switched hands, and cut the other palm.

She lay flat on her back, arms stretched out at her sides, palms to the air, and let them begin. They needed to eat. They needed to drink. And if she needed to die, then so be it.

They supped away, drinking from her blood, silencing their screams. She felt each one of their heartbeats, sensed the calming of their soul, and let herself be eaten, her blood their wine, and, with the ferocity of their jaws now gaining energy, her body their bread. Like piranha they latched on to her, their appetites insatiable. She was being hollowed out by the tiny infants, and felt a bitter coldness, like waves of ice washing over her. Lying in *The Cemetery of the Innocents*, she was sure this would also be her own grave.

This is suicide. Letting myself die. Just like Keagan's dad. Just like Jesus.

Next time she opened her eyes, her body would be aflame in Hell, and she'd be face to face with the devil.

She heard footsteps, felt breathing, an explosion of warmth, as if a star had fallen from the sky. The fiery glow of something ancient, as old as the universe, beat back the icy chill. She forced open her eyes and looked up at the face of Jesus. He stood over her, glowing with love, waiting, but doing nothing. He was watching her being eaten alive, bearing witness to her death.

Why have you abandoned me? she thought, sure that he must hear her thoughts, expecting him to lift her up and take her into the heavens, but instead he remained indifferent. He did nothing. She was abandoned, and would die feeding her spawn. Her sacrifice would be their myth, this meal their religion.

Just as she felt herself slip into death, the infants stopped their feast. Their heads swiveled, their cheeks dripping with blood. Jesus spread his arms wide, and as if by a magnet, the children were summoned to his body. They crawled with a new swiftness to the Lord, took one small bite at his clay-like skin, and then became a part of his body. She could see their tiny eyes inside his flesh of Communion wafers for a split second, and then they were gone, taken into his bloodstream, into his bread, all her children gone to Jesus.

They were loved, they were cared for, they would never want or be lonely. She closed her eyes and let the oblivion have her.

Chapter Nine: Keagan

KEAGAN KNEW NOTHING would be the same after the gunshots blew apart his world, once again on Halloween night. He had to hide everything, including the truth, which nobody really wanted to know, and the tiny creature, who he could house in his backpack.

Before the ambulance arrived, and before walking off into the night, Jesus had held the tiny, wriggling infant in his arms. The infant was human, but born premature, with tiny fingers and an aching hunger. Jesus promptly pulled a slice of flesh off his forearm and gave the baby Communion. The puckering for food stopped and Keagan sensed that it felt peace. Jesus walked off towards the church, and Keagan put the tiny infant away in his backpack.

The police arrived to Keagan's house, (he recognized one of them from the year before), and an ambulance took his momma's body. The wheels of the stretcher squeaked under the weight of the cadaver, while the flashing red lights circled in the air and neighbors gathered.

Keagan was taken to the police station, where he talked to social workers who drank coffee from white Styrofoam cups. Then they gave him a pillow and a blanket and an office chair where he could fall asleep, which he did after making sure his new baby was safe in his backpack.

Some days later, Keagan was a foster child in a foster home. The mom and dad were Catholic proper, and ate dinner at the same time every night. He had his own bedroom, his own closet to hide things inside, and a set of clothes for each day of the week. His older foster brother punched him in the stomach when the parents weren't looking. They took him to see psychiatrists who asked him if he poisoned his mom, and tell him he won't get in trouble for telling the truth.

Nobody gets the truth, though. Nobody.

They never found Jesus. He was walking the earth somewhere, perhaps enjoying Halloween at another house each year. Keagan misses him, but takes comfort that his foster family is Catholic and brings him to church. Each Sunday he goes to Communion and collects wafers: from the priest, to his mouth, to his tongue, to his closet. Once in a while, he cuts himself, and adds a bit of his own blood to the collection of wafers.

He's building his own Jesus in the bedroom closet, where the tiny child lives that he has kept hidden all this time. He has named the child Faith, just a little version of his friend. Keagan was the father, Faith the mother, and the Holy Spirit shined inside this little being. When Keagan feels his life grow dark, when his spirit blackens and he feels lost and alone, he knows he can't kill himself. He has too much to live for.

And promise me you'll never have a child. It's a burden to have a meaning in life and not be able to kill oneself proper.

Another promise he broke. Like taking Communion.

And he'll keep breaking these promises in secret, in his foster care home, for the infant known as Faith is growing hungry, and will need a true piece of Jesus to survive.

THE LAST BUG-CHASER

We carry the arc in our blood. Us Gideons. Your bodies on earth are just the vessels.

My ancestors took a one-way passage after we saw the timelines with multiple extinction points for your planet. Your race would never take its rightful place in the celestial community without us. We see it. We feel it. You carry a cerebral goldmine wrapped up in that pink brain of yours. Once your species learns how to tap into its power, the lifeforce inside will explode into a new consciousness and join us in the heavens.

Some of you have had a brief glimpse, with your psychedelic drugs, with your prayers and meditations, but you mistake it for madness rather than harness its potential.

This will never happen if you're wiped out by bugs first.

It started when we carried Noah to the rainbow. Your books tell of a flood, what you may never know is that flood was not of water but of viral devastation. You needed our plasma to survive. When the animals dispersed two by two, so did we, evolving in mad dashes. We were there for the black death. The great plagues in Russia and London. For Ebola and Zika and Covid-19. It takes time to make sure the bugs were neutralized on your scales of measurement, but just a blip in ours.

Our blood is full of splendor, alive and healing, with the wonders of big-bang starshine, but your bodily cages keep us trapped. These visceral bodies are a prison. This chaotic society of yours built on passions of the flesh we now understand, for we are stuck inside skin and bone just like you.

This was a sacrifice we had to make to save your planet and blend in. The reason we had to hide among you, well disguised, was made clear when you felt threatened and attacked our hive. Stuck in your bodies, we had no defense when you invaded our lair. Now most of us are dead, some of us are missing.

See what you did?

I've lost contact with the elder Gideons, my mission is now solitary. I am the only one left, far as I can tell. I have one insidious bug to chase.

So I sit and wait outside the double set of doors that guard the hospital floor. When the electric door beeps and opens, slow as a moat, the vestibule in the middle is a little purgatory that reminds me of the butterfly cages in your zoos. Those beautiful bugs with mosaic wings.

Health professionals walk out the locked wing, and I try not to examine them too directly as I look for a crack in the defense

I am like your legendary Dorothy from Oz, traveling to this strange land, and trying to slip inside the witch's castle.

I pace, looking preoccupied, glancing up to the ceiling as if answers to everything that ails me is stuck above. I act the role of a distressed person that your race likes to avoid. Once in a while, I let out a sigh.

Patience.

Medical staff don't suspect a thing as they exit, ready to return to the places they come from.

A woman walks out. She smells of sanitizer and disinfectant, but she's not the right one, so I wait. I sense the infected patient inside. My mouth waters, my soul waters, but I wait.

If only the others in my tribe could see my work.

Kyra, you should stay away. let Flynn do the work

Fucking Flynn. You think Flynn could pull off the *fuck of death* with this patient they guard inside?

Flynn didn't have to earn anything. Born on third base, thinks he hit a triple. Living off the legend of his father, who contracted the Swine Flu so early on and became a legend.

Flynn was nothing like his father, a direct elder descendant. His hair ridiculous. That fucking curl hanging over his forehead all the time. A question mark on his skull, like—is there really a brain inside this pretty face?

Flynn wasn't motivated for the Gideon mission, he loved the attention, and it was his interview in the New Yorker that outed us to investigators. "The Erotic Drive of HIV Bug Chasers" they called it, with his picture on front, and I'm sure that lead to the raid. Ridiculous. Everything about him. Ridiculous.

The way he gloated in the pleasures of being human.

A beep from the door. A woman exits. She's my height, nearly, and a hair color that seems close.

She hits the elevator button and waits, and I make my way to the stairwell. I dash down the stairs, out to the first floor, and she's just getting out of the elevator. I walk as if her shadow at sunset.

She moves with weight. She's carrying too much. She's seen too much. I follow her through the hallways, to the parking garage, and I know she senses me. Slightly uncomfortable, so I switch from hidden follower to eager fan. Time to make my move. I rush up alongside her.

"Excuse me. I'm sorry. Excuse me. I just want to thank you. Please, let me thank you." I look into her tired eyes. "I don't know how to say this but I have to thank you for all the work you people do. You must be so tired."

Part of me felt she deserved the truth. That all her efforts were useless. They can't contain this bug. They won't. The patient they tend to is certainly the most viral—closet to death is always the strongest virus—but this bug is ready to blow the illusions of safety right off the planet. Without my intervention, soon the planet's atmosphere will stink of rotting bodies.

The woman gives me a polite glance. She doesn't want praise. She lives in a private world of servitude, and I breathe it in deeply, hoping to inhale her exhales, to feel each molecule of her scent in my lungs.

"Thank you kindly," was her curt answer.

She looks away. *God, she has people waiting for her.* Loved ones who would never know the true sacrifice she is about to make.

"Really. I mean it," I say. "I lost my parent to the virus. I know the sickness you've seen. I appreciate you and all you've done. Can I give you a hug?"

Her hair seems to stand on end, porcupine quills sensing a threat, but she is about to succumb, to get it over so she could move on. A smile escapes her mouth, just a touch, and then she stops herself, because there is no reason to smile. There is only death and waiting for death and what to do after death. A wave of dead bodies getting higher, gathering momentum, and then crashing onto shore.

Your planet would face mass extinction if I don't do this.

I pulled her tightly as I could, my cheek near hers, every cell on her is tingling, releasing its own stored history. I sensed a 16-hour shift. I sensed the scent of saline solutions in IV bags. I could feel the memories of looking at patients dying of the virus.

If only I could soak the virus from her pores, I wouldn't have to do this, but there's not a trace of the bug.

I lift one foot and place my heel behind her leg. I let go of my embrace around her back, and with one motion, pushed on her chest, swooping my leg to make her go falling straight backwards. The look of surprise on her face in slow motion, questioning me, questioning all of humankind—the ultimate betrayal by someone hiding hurtful intentions under the guise of gratitude.

She will understand, like all of you will understand, once her spirit escapes the dead carcass.

Her head had smashes to the ground, a strange echo in this parking structure, the sound of a melon hitting concrete.

Her eyes close. I can't tell if she is dead, but I do sense blood. I bend over, place a palm on her cheek and whisper how sorry I am. Her only response is blood puddling under her cracked skull. It pools on the ground as if I'd just drilled for oil. I dab into the blood with a finger, and place it in my mouth for a taste, coating my tongue with her blood. Nothing. No virus inside, just clean, healthy blood of the dying woman.

Her body weighs much more in death than in life. I drag her inside her car. Changing clothes in the back seat is tight.

I dig in her purse and take the employee badge. Now I am Dorothy disguised as a guard going into the castle, only Dorothy had friends. I have none. All of my tribe is gone from the raid, most of them killed, but Flynn has gone missing.

Fucking Flynn.

With his love for the spot light, his need to be noticed, his rants in private about how we should go public and get credit for our species. If he were the last one left, he'd have been captured by whoever it was that had thinned our herd, but not me. I avoided intersections, because facial recognition cameras are everywhere. I wear hats. I resist urges to even say hi or make eye contact in public. I live in hotels. I take out credit cards under fake names. And I wait for moments like this.

We should have traveled more. We should have sanctioned Flynn to house arrest and held a tribunal. We should have lived in cells, not in one spot.

Should haves didn't matter. There was only me—the last Gideon bug chaser, looking for the virus that would kill your planet and a gaping hole in future celestial communities of the divine.

My curse in this body is the insatiable drive to contract this bug.

Back into the hospital, I ride the elevator to floor nine. I'm an employee now, someone who knows their way around. I keep my chin to my chest on the ride up, as if bowing, waiting for the doors to open. My soul is a thunderous tempest of anticipation, crashing waves of energy against jagged rocks, but on the surface, I'm calm.

I stepped through, walking without a glance to anyone to my side.

The badge was on a retractable lanyard, and I pulled the plastic card with the dying woman's face on it. After a swipe, a green light that whispers *Yes*, the door swings open, and I hide my delight. I fill myself with the sad purpose of saving others.

I'm in the vestibule, and the door closes behind me. I am in purgatory, and walk the five yards to the next door, the badge swipes again, and I'm in.

I've been on quarantine units before. I know the first stop is protective equipment. Gown, facemask, eye protection. I follow another worker seamlessly, mimicking her as she gathered supplies from PPE station, not making eye contact. I'm important

Harder to see me under the layers of plastic and fabric and mask and goggles, easier to hide the true nature of my soul, of my blood, of my immune system.

I know typical shift changes. New staff will come in at 11 pm, but they are nothing compared to the power of the virus. I can sense it, smell it, feel the heat. I'm at its epicenter, like I've dove into a volcano, trying to stop the eruption of deaths that awaits.

God, I've felt many bugs in my life, but never anything as powerful as this.

I know my way around these hallways, I might as well have been blind. The IV tubes leading from machines into veins—that's me. Catheters taking in waste—that's me. Ventilators making lungs breathe—that's me. I wear the PPE like a diver wearing scuba gear, but I can breathe under water.

With each step, I feel it getting closer. Stronger, hotter. I can hear the virus, organic strands in a frenzy. The chemical makeup of this virus differs only slightly from the very blood of my species. I turn to his room.

I'm inside and I see him. Intubated. Plastic drapes cover the sides of his bed, double layers. His skin is yellow, blotchy, sweaty, feverish. Lymph nodes are swollen like two golf balls stuck in his neck. I can feel the fever, and the room starts to buzz.

I'm a fly and he's raw meat in a dumpster.

I feel the urges of your human body and its visceral passions take over, and I want to mount him on first sight.

Does he notice me? His eyes seem open, a slit with just a hint of pupil. I don't know if he's awake, but the virus inside surely is. The virus could feel me. Sense me. I hear the electrons spinning inside the genetic code, strands of DNA surrounded by a protein coat.

I hide in the closet, squeezed inside, and hear nurses walk in and out of the room. I wait for the darkest of hours, when nurses who didn't sleep during the day promise not to doze off, but they do. That's when I open the closet door slowly and my flesh gets goosebumps. My skin covered with a cold, clammy sweat. The host sleeps peacefully, but the virus is awake. I can feel it penetrate his capillaries, rushing through his blood stream, microscopic cells in a frenzy, just children on a roller coaster.

I remove my PPE, peeling it off like a snake shedding skin, baring my soul, zippering off my flesh. I stand completely naked, a mix of heat and moisture rising, and each skin cell is craving to be touched. I'm a dancing, sweaty woman on ecstasy at one of your raves. I'm a shark ready to feast on a bloody prey.

I'm the last bug chaser.

I pull back the plastic shades that surround the patient, and immerse myself into the cloud. This man is maybe 60 years old, already fragile before the virus, but now it is the virus that keeps him alive. The glue of his soul. I place a palm on the flesh of his cheek, and feel the bug inside rush through.

I want to lick some green mucus from his nostrils. I want to place my tongue into his mouth and lick saliva from his tongue. All of that works to catch the bug and contract the virus, but none works as certain as *the Fuck of Death.* God did I need it.

Can this man get erect?

Only by a bug chaser. One who knows to rub him and incite the invaders inside, and as I remove the gown to the side, I take him flaccid in my hands, but soon, the burning in his body spikes. The fever makes him sweat and I lick the salty flesh. I hate these pleasures of humans that I succumb to.

His eyes open, they are not him, they are the virus. It knows I've come for it. I can see it burn a reddish orange.

False to say he enters me, true to say I engulf him, sliding him into me and feeling every bit of his raging infection as I grind my hips and fuck.

God does this one burn in places that have never felt a fire, inciting red passion. My hips gyrate on top of him. Rhythmic. Dance-like. His eyes widen and look up at me. He knows he's dying, his soul is infected, like black mold poisoning his structure until his body becomes more infection than person.

But he'll die with me on top of him. A lover from a faraway celestial body and unlike any other he's seen. I know what I look like in these moments—quivering flesh, electric touch— a succubus of sorts—and he can do nothing when I bend down to plunge my teeth into the swollen lymph nodes on his neck. I taste his blood.

He swells inside me ready to explode.

I come up for air, my lips soaked in red. Everything moist and dripping with the wetness of sex and viral fluids and bugs swimming frantically about. I tighten and squeeze every last drop out of him, *God,* I moan to myself as we both reach orgasmic climax. I want to scream to the glorious heavens.

Maybe I do scream, because my skull is vibrating with the noise.

I am the last bug-chaser, and I am patient zero now. The plasma in my veins attacks and battles the virus in an instant. The blood of my species mutates inside me. Once my transition is complete, in just three day's time, I will shed my blood for others. I will pass on my immunity to your frail species, and it will grow exponentially. Just a breath of air exhaled from my lungs into yours will create immunity. Just the touch of my skin will leave traces of my DNA to soak inside others.

We are the saviors, the bug chasers. Like your Jesus curing the lepers. Your science is nothing compared to our species who are saving your sadly maladaptive human race, who would surely have perished without us.

I wipe blood off my chin, lick it with my fingers, and swallow. The man is dead. Like a slight wind coming from the East, I feel his soul leave his body, and the peace inside when all is still. What could be mistaken for a grin is spread on his face. His flesh will soon grow cold, but my own body is burning. Chemical explosions erupt inside my veins, and my chest cavity is a steam engine.

I need to leave. I have to get out the door. Machines start beeping, people will come. I turn to the door, but it's blocked.

A shadow has appeared, someone watching me.

I squint through the greyness of the room. I make out a question mark curl swirl on the man's forehead. I smell the scent of my race. A fellow bug chaser. I am not alone. My kind has found me.

It's Flynn.

"You did it. I knew it. We knew it. Come with me, I've got people waiting. We've got to go."

"People. Who? Daxon? Penelope?" (Our two leaders, God they were beautiful.)

"Better. I got people who know us. Who know *this*. Let's move. Staff are coming."

I move with the beautiful buzz of the virus inside me. My chin wet with blood, my womb wet with bugs, my heart buzzing with electric blood, and my immune system in chain reaction explodes through my veins. Flynn wraps me in a patient's white robe, and we move down the hallway.

Two steps out the door, and nurses run into the room. They've known death before, they expected this death, it is no surprise. I have this urge to touch each person we pass, an insatiable thirst to spread what's inside me and scatter it like dandelion seeds, but the time is not yet. Our blood takes three days to be ready to spread.

Flynn has answers to what happened to my tribe that I need to hear. He escorts me out, and we move through the hallways, and suddenly I'm Dorothy, fleeing the castle with witch's broom in hand.

We ride the elevator down alone without a word. I have so many questions

We walk the desolate hallways to the exit. A few somber families huddle in hallway, trapped in the wet blanket of no sleep and deep grief. My bare feet patter on the floor. My flesh still wet. Moist.

And the click, click, click, of footsteps behind me.

Two men in suits follow us. I sense them tracking me. They feel cold and invasive against my body which is hot, feverish, sweating under this robe, ready to set it on fire.

I'm in the middle of a triangle. Flynn next to me, two men behind.

This is all wrong. This is a march I don't want to take.

Flynn opens the door to outside the hospital, and my complicity ends. I bust into a sprint out the door, legs churning furiously.

I dash down the cement pathway leading to the parking lot. My legs propel me with ferocity, my body full of boiling blood and a steam whistle cracks the silence of the night.

I'll escape this trap, whatever it is. I'll live on without the answers that Flynn can give me, and I'll spread my immunity to your race so that you may evolve, my sacrifice never known to future generations.

But I don't get far. My bare feet can't move fast enough and I am tackled from behind. I go sprawling on the cement and the two men take control of my limbs. They have me, and Flynn stands over us as the third captor.

A black Lincoln navigator pulls up curbside and the door opens. This is a kidnapping.

They push me into the back seat, Flynn next to me, the others in front. The door slams shut and the driver takes off with tires squealing.

I'm not in a car, I'm in a cage, and I want to scream questions. I want to curse Flynn for whatever scandalous move he's making here, but that feels like what he wants. He wants me scared, pleading, a helpless damsel, not a queen carrying an elixir in her blood that will to save these humans after I harrow hell for three days.

Flynn's wearing a fitted suit and leather shoes. He's so happy being human.

I was not a cherished Gideon passenger in this car—I was the cargo.

"I'm sorry. I really am," Flynn says, talking with his hands like a salesman. "You don't understand what is happening here. You never did."

"Where are they, where are the rest of us?" I finally ask in a voice that no longer sounds like mine, because my body is transforming, quivering, a butterfly trying to bust out of its cocoon.

"They were taken care of. They didn't understand. They don't see the world in the new way. Not in the way MEDGENICS does."

"MEDGENICS? That's who this is?"

The men rustle up front. Then return their gazes forward.

MEDGENICS is a monster big pharm conglomerate, who owned half of congress and all of the president.

"They are helping us. We are helping them"

"*Them*? What is this rotten hell you've dragged me too? God damn you Flynn."

"They helped me understand how precious we are, you and I. How we deserve to live better than we have been. We don't need to suffer. You think any other Gideons would live in these bodies and not fully enjoy them, never a moment of relief from this curse? We can live our mission here and enjoy the full experience these human forms can offer."

My skin is pulsating, beaming with a reddish hue from the heat. The robe is sticky and clammy from sweat oozing from my pores. I want to undress and let my body do its magic, and in three days I'll have the vaccine in my veins.

"You can't imagine the delicious life I've led since realizing we need not chase bugs in the same manner any longer. We need alliances. We need transitions. To adapt. When others refused, they were sacrificed. Unable to adapt. Like the virus in our bodies, no longer a threat."

"You killed them all, didn't you?"

"I didn't harm a single one. I only tried to convince them of the truth, but they were stubborn. They are not like you and I. You know why we had such quarrels together? It is because you and I are the same. We are part of the same circle, the yin-yang forever attached."

Anger fills me, and then tears. Salty hot tears on my cheek that sizzle off my burning skin when I imagined the faces of my slaughtered tribe. I remembered their lives. I felt their lost souls. They were killed by the very species who I was supposed to be saving. *Maybe your race doesn't deserve to be saved*, a truth I denied but needed to admit. Why not let you suck the life out of each other? You humans are the most dangerous beast in any zoo. The most beautiful are the bugs with wings. Lock the people up, and let the bugs fly free.

"We are going to take you somewhere comfortable. I know what you are going through right now, and sitting in this car is no way to transform. We are just chemical labs, you and I. Walking, breathing, chemical labs. And when you are done, MEDGENICS will pull the immunity from your body and make their own vaccine. They will compensate you with riches and rewards for your human body that others can only dream of. And with every new bug, just more riches."

"Hell no."

"Please don't be like that. Please don't. You'll not want to say no. Trust me. I saw what they do when they hear *no*. What they did to the others. I said I didn't hurt them, but they did. They do. They have manufactured bugs they can put inside us that will react with our blood and melt our skin from the insides. Slowly, of course, over the course of weeks. Daxon cried. Can you believe that? *Daxon*. Didn't think it possible. I watched a bit, but I had to turn away. You've no idea what kind of pain you can feel inside this human shell."

We bumped along the highway. Traffic started to fill the streets during the morning rush hour. Headlights pierced the predawn darkness, cars speeding and packed together. The road rushed by under our feet, probably at 90 miles an hour or more. This crew doesn't get pulled over by police, and if they did, it wouldn't matter. They know people. *They are people*, and they speed along with the entitlement that comes with their industry. I can smell the experimented animals on them, the clinical trials gone wrong but then covered up. Even if they control the vaccine, I know how MEDGENICS works. They will let their brothers and sisters die to make demand sky-rocket and profits soar.

They are everything that is wrong with this species. The butterfly garden doors need to be busted open.

"Just you and I are left then, right Flynn?" I ask.

"Just you and I," he answers.

"This bug is so special," I said with sultry tongue. "I can't tell you how good this makes my body feel. *God if you only knew*. You might think you know, but you don't… not really. I'm on fire. I need to be touched… I can't wait any more. Someone has to touch me."

I pull the robe down, exposing my breasts and my quivering flesh. Everything burns from the cauldron of chemical explosions in my bloodstream.

"You want a taste?"

The men in front turn their heads. The temperature of the car changes.

"I know you want to touch me Flynn. I need you to touch me."

I open my body towards him, legs wide as they will go in this back seat, arms spread open, chest forward.

Everything accelerates—my blood, my heart, the rushing concrete just underneath me. Flynn can't resist. He slides into me, and I suck him in like the swirling Charybdis. I embrace him with both arms and pull his face to my breast. He can feel the bug inside, a new kind of mother's milk. His whole body presses against mine until we are fused together as one.

We are the yin-yang he promised, his flesh stuck against mine.

I give him a Judas kiss, put one hand around his neck, the other behind me on the car door handle, and I pull, praying the door will open. Such relief when I hear the door click, and just as it cracks open, I hold his body against my own.

When I lean backwards and plunge, I take him with me to the street below.

I catch one flash image of his shocked face before hitting the pavement at 90 miles an hour. My head hits first, my back second, his body next.

We rolled with such speed the cement rips my flesh, skinning me alive. Bones split apart, fracturing in half and the jagged edges protrude from my limbs. Road rash rips at me with such ferocity I can hear the flesh being shred. My skull is bouncing, fracturing with each impact.

My suicide is full of pain, the price I pay for the transformation from life to death. Mission aborted, and soon I will rejoin the souls of Gideons in the afterlife.

Cars swerve and hit each other. Flynn gets drilled by a truck, just a rag doll smashed by the grill of an 18-wheeler. Tires bounce over him like he's a human speed bump, finally depositing his body behind. The next car hits him again and his carcass gets stuck underneath, dragging him on the pavement.

Flynn becomes a 50-yard smear of blood and entrails.

My body pinballs from fender to fender, bouncing off cars with drum-beat thuds, until it flies in the air and I splat like a bug on a windshield. My last gaze is at a family of three inside the car. One of your nuclear families: mom, dad, child in the back.

They will die soon. I see it in a flash. The dad will get infected and the virus will turn his body into an oozing sprinkler of infectious fluids, passing the bug on to the mom, who promises to keep her girl safe, but she can't. I see swollen lymph nodes on all of them. I see mucus. I hear coughs and groans until they die from respiratory failure.

I see my own cremation after I'm scraped from this pavement, and the viral death of millions.

The lights of your humanity will go dim after a decade of devastation. Your species will go extinct and your planet will start anew without humans. Hard to argue that it wasn't for the best. Gideons will watch from the stars and wait to see if a new species evolves that is worthy of our aid.

Mask of Sanity

"Eva Terklowski killed herself last night," said Ms. Haack, charge nurse of Sharepoint psychiatric hospital. "Successful suicide."

"What? How?"

"Household supplies. She injected bleach into her IV port, and then drank some drain cleaner. Her sister found her dead. After all of the ways she's tried to kill herself, that was what finally worked."

I imagined the little clouds of bleach invading the flow of her veins, the internal bleeding, and then the chest pains when it reached her heart. But when that didn't kill her, she must have moved about the house in her wheelchair looking for something else, found the drain cleaner, and drank the blue liquid through her already foaming lips. Cutting herself with sharp objects had always been her choice in the past, but this cut her up from the insides, and now she was finally dead.

"Her poor sister. Oh my God."

"Yes, I know," said nurse Haack. "sometimes these things are understandable."

It was understandable, I thought, but would not say out loud. As her psychiatrist, I had told Eva as much, and how, after eight times trying to commit suicide, she must have felt even more helpless. What I didn't say is that many times I looked at her wrecked body as really just a reflection of my own insides, her face just mine unmasked. Eva seemed to know my secrets. Now, despite numerous combinations of medications I'd prescribed, her depression seemed untreatable.

"You know they will want us to go through her chart," Ms. Haack said, "and make sure it's been documented well, in case there's an investigation. "

"I know, I know."

This was the third completed suicide by ex-patients this week. Max Davis hung himself the same day he was discharged, and Lori Engle slit her own arm at least 47 times before bleeding to death. Either they finally got better at it, or they finally really wanted to die. Or I finally fucked up so bad and did the wrong thing that pushed them over the edge.

I stood frozen thinking of my dead ex-patients, unsure of what to do next, while the flurry at the nurses' station buzzed all around me. This place was like the center of the beehive, dishing out medications, documenting every shift, following orders and chain of commands. Just moments ago, an agitated patient had to receive a Haldol cocktail injected into their muscle to keep him calm. And for the most dangerous of patients, the Haldol cocktail is followed up by an hour locked up inside the seclusion room.

Sometimes I felt like the only difference between me and my patients was my mask of sanity. Something I pulled on so tight it would never come off, but underneath it all, I envied the sense of desperation, the extremities of living but wanting to die. Life is a gift, sanity not a given, and to stave off the madness is something I took as serious as one could, but how often in my private thoughts had I wished I could dive into the same insanity I try to treat. To feel what it was like to slice into the blue pulsating vein in my neck, an exacto-knife splitting down the jugular and that brief second before life left me when I watched my blood spray on the walls of my home.

But tonight, I was having Dawn come over, and it was moments like these that made me work hard to keep my mask of sanity on tight. She gave me hope I could find something to live for.

Dawn was a pharmaceutical representative who had been dishing out samples of her new anti-depressant drug, QUINZAPINE, the *best cure for depression when everything else has failed.* "I take it too," she confessed. She gave me enough doses to get most of my caseload started on the new drug, and filled my office with stationary, flashlight pens, and IPhone covers with *Quinzapine* written across it. Tonight, when I suspected I would see her undressed for the first time, I wondered if I would find *Quinzapine* tattooed on her breast.

I pulled into my driveway and noticed the lawn. I had not cut it in a week and it looked like an unkept vacant lot, with the tiny wheat-like split atop each green blade. This was the house of a man who might not have his shit together, who let his clients die, who heard about them dying then had sex with the pharmaceutical reps that same night. All the while wearing some fake psychiatrist mask. It would take a well-crafted dinner, and a freshly shaved face to fool Dawn into believing my mask was true.

I clean up well, and I can cook. Over dinner, Dawn kept her lips pursed in a smug smile, like she was holding in a laugh, an inside joke between her and her own thoughts. Dinner was shrimp scampi on a bed of linguine.

"They come in threes," I said during an awkward silence, hoping I sounded mysterious.

She kept chewing and was not impressed. She apparently didn't like parsley and was picking the tiny green bits off.

"Three patients successfully suicided right after they discharged. All in one week," I said to thicken the bait. "I know it is bound to happen, but three in one week is the kind of thing that makes you question your judgment."

"You have poor judgment?" she either asked or accused.

"Of course not, I have wonderful judgment, just... my judgement can't be too bad, because I'm sitting here with you."

A perk of being a doctor. Free pens and a night with the Pharm Rep.

"Dosaging. It's all about the dosage. And the titration is important."

"I am aware."

"No, you are not, because you are asking me why these patients who were on Quinzapine tried to kill themselves. Then again, maybe, just maybe they were on the right dose, but it just doesn't matter. Everything we do is irrelevant. 90 percent of it at least. Only 10 percent of what we do matters, we just aren't sure which 10, so we do 100 percent and wait."

This was going down a weird path. "Get that research funded," I quipped and gulped some wine. It went right to my sweat pores and beaded out my skin.

"No more talk of suicide," I declared, "it might wreck this moment."

"Or moments to come," she said, butter glistening from her lips. "Don't think I'm not thinking the same thing as you are. But… I have rules, you know, for the first time I sleep with a man," she indeed seemed to be reading my mind.

"I'm quite certain I can accommodate."

"I stay over. I will not leave tonight. I need to wake up with you in the morning."

"You are invited to sleepover. Breakfast will be even better than dinner."

She twirled a piece of linguine in her fork, spinning it fast and efficient, before lifting it off the plate and then stabbing down on a piece of shrimp. The impaled crustacean dangled and then she filled her mouth with the tiny beast. Her lips glistened with butter and spread into a smirk. I watched her chew.

"Our last meal before *La Petit Mort*," she said.

"Another rule?"

"Not exactly. Just an inevitable tragedy of our condition. La Petit Mort. *A little death*. Sex is just a little death. Parts of us die. You ready for that?"

I certainly was, and as expected, my mask was pulled off and only my primal self remained once she joined my bed. The sex was exquisite, primitive, and probably didn't pull back my mask as much as burned it off of me. The heat of my body made it sizzle and bubble so that so stuck to my skin like dripping candle wax. Everything seemed to be burning with passion, and the flame melted us together in a pile of flesh. This was a treasure of a woman in my bed and I did not want the night to end.

I watched her go to sleep but I could not sleep myself. I knew she would share my bed again many times if I handled this right. I would come to know her quirks, I would explore and find all her sweet spots, and a thousand little deaths awaited.

A slit of blue moonlight shone through the window shade and made Dawn's flesh glow. The moonbeam was a dawn of rising happiness in my life that I hoped could last a long time. Maybe forever.

Knock. Pause. *Knock*. Pause. *Knock*.

There was something rapping against my bedroom door. I held my breath to keep everything silent to see if the noise was real.

Knock, pause. *Knock*, pause.

My heart thumped, louder than the door's knocking, and I got up in silence with plans to protect my sleeping Dawn. I stood in front of the door, waiting to snatch the handle and fling it open, but the noise had faded. There was nothing to hear but the whoosh of blood in my ears.

I had imagined it all.

I turned to go back to Dawn's warm body in my bed when the noises returned but this time with power. BANG-BANG-BANG. My hand flew to the handle and I swung the door open.

The shrimp fettucine in my stomach swirled and I got ready to vomit. I put a hand up to my mouth when I felt bile rise up my throat but then swallowed it down.

Eva Terklowski was sitting there before me in her wheelchair, but she was not the same. Foam on her swollen lips bubbled, and wounds like acne surrounded her mouth. Her dead skin had turned grey except for blotches of purple bedsores. Her eyes were vacant in the dark, and unblinking. I could not tell if there was a pupil.

"I did it, my good Doctor, I did it," she said. "I finished the job. Now tell me; why is it you deserve to live?"

I shut the door fast, and the noise made Dawn stir. She moved her legs lightly across each other, like a cricket playing music under the moon. One arm slipped farther under the pillow. She remained asleep.

Oh God, don't fuck this up. I'm dreaming. I've gone mad.

I opened the door again, and there Eva still was, sitting in her wheelchair. Her scraggly hair, like that from an old doll, shot out of her head, each strand seemed alive and hissing like a snake. Her fingers just tentacles resting on the wheels. How many times had she sat before me in my office, telling me how painful her life was, how she cursed each day she woke, and only a dreamless sleep brought any reprieve. Each suicide attempt just another failure, the many times she was charcoaled and vomited, the black bile arising like her soul. Each failed attempt resulted in another hospital stay. Her last few times in my office she'd sit with empty gaze and empty words.

But in my bedroom doorway, she'd found her voice.

"Your house, Doctor, is same as everyplace. Always making it hard for the mobility impaired to get through the door. You're an ableist, doctor, someone who thinks those who can't do what you do should suffer. You pretend to help, but look—I can barely get into the same room with you."

The doorway was indeed skinny.

She is alive. Call 911, get medical attention, save her.

But this was not a truly live person. This was something different. Something bigger. A visit from beyond, since I could hear other spirits moving about the house, something ghostly. From the bathroom, I heard the faucet running in spurts, turning on and off, on and off. Light shone through the crack in the door. Someone was inside.

I put my hand on Eva's wheelchair and gave it a tender slide away, but not tender enough to stop her from calling me a *stupid shrink fuck*, and saying *if my legs could move, I would trip you up and make you fall into hell.*

I walked past her to the bathroom. I needed water. A mirror, for surely the mask of sanity was off now and I'd see the real me for the first time. I pushed the bathroom door but it hit something and would open no further. A foot was in the way.

I peered through the crack and saw an arm in the sink. Up and down the arm were dozens of slashes. The faucet streamed like a waterfall down the arm and blood was pouring forth from the ragged, bloody limb as if it was a chocolate fondue. But the owner of the arm didn't think it was enough, for they continued to slice away.

I winced when I heard the noise, *Whack,* and saw the slash of a razor blade cut into the arm. I heard the shriek of the person inside, a woman who had no clue I was there. I hadn't yet seen her face but I could smell the thick plasma in the air. It stuck to my nostrils, coated my insides, and before I could slam the door shut, she snuck a look around the corner.

I was face to face with Lori Engle. Ex-patient of Sharepoint hospital, dead as of five days ago.

"Successful suicide," Lori announced with pride. "Like you said, doctor, If I really wanted to die, I would have cut myself more, not just a superficial slash, but multiple slices, down the vein. Now I know. Thanks Doc."

My heart thumped a drumbeat in my chest and pressure built in my head. I pulled the door shut. My vision was fading, bile still rising. If I threw up now all my insides would come out and I'd bust apart forever. *Got to keep it together, now more than ever.*

Lori Engle was someone I thought was histrionic, who feigned suicide just to create a crisis. I had challenged her on her repeated non-lethal suicide attempts and even asked her, "if you were to kill yourself, who do you think would find your body?" hoping to discover the source of her anger.

She'd said, "nobody would find me, I'm all alone." But she was wrong, because I'd found her with slashed wrists in my own bathroom.

I needed to get back to Dawn and the safety of the bedroom. I quickly returned, and found Eva had squeezed her wheelchair through the doorway, and was sitting bedside by Dawn who remained sleeping.

"Shhhh, you are going to wake her up?" said Eva with a finger pressed to her lips. "She is a fine specimen. Who wouldn't want to lay their hands on her?" Eva held out a pointy, delicate finger ready to touch Dawn's exposed flesh.

In a flash I grabbed a hold of the wheelchair handles and pulled Eva out of the room. Her body jolted from the motion and I waited for her to cry out but she did not. We were down the hallway, past the bleeding body of Lori, and I planned to dump Eva's body on the front porch where the whole world could see that she was truly here, truly alive. Just a call to the cops away from having everything back where it was supposed to be. Flashing lights and then an ambulance ride and all would be restored.

But something in the hallway blocked my passage. My forehead slammed into the hard plastic of boots, and a set of legs swayed in the air like wind chimes. I looked up, and staring down at me was the face of Max Davis, his eyes wide open, his tongue stuck out of his mouth, and his head hung slack. A noose hung from the light fixture. Max had used it as his hanging tree.

"Just had to kick the ladder to get this one right, Doc. But I got it this time. Thanks man."

Screams gathered in my mouth but my brain was too confused to let them rip free. Laughter from all three of them echoed in my head. *Just in my head. That was it.* Their dead bodies seemed real, but they were not real. Not permanent. A manic dream.

Max had Major Depressive Disorder with Psychosis, resulting in command hallucinations telling him he needed to kill himself. I'd prescribed Zoloft and Abilify, titrated dosages with some great success but then switched to Quinzapine. This seemed to work even better, but there he was, hanging from my light fixture.

"Let me down, Doc. I want to come down now. I'm alright now. Please, cut me down."

I didn't want him down. It was safer with him hanging there. Three of my patients were in the house now, but there was only one person I wanted to save. *Dawn*, who was in the bedroom still sleeping.

I headed back to be with her, I needed Dawn close, and so it seemed did my patients. Lori had wheeled Eva's chair into the bedroom, a trail of blood like mop soap behind them. I followed the trail bedside. Lori stood there smiling while blood dripped from her wounds. Eva's skin seemed to be decomposing more each second, her body a meal not fit for a vulture.

They peered over Dawn's golden smooth flesh as if paying homage to a sleeping queen.

"Don't you touch her," I said, but that is exactly what she did. Lori started to trace a finger along her thigh, slow and sensual, me just a frozen witness. Dawn stirred at the soft caress as if it was from her lover in the morning, not a dead woman with no blood left in her body.

I had to get Dawn out of there.

I reached down to collect her in my arms, a hero ready to whisk his princess to safety. One arm was under her, then two. Just then her eyes opened and looked into mine. I started to lift, but got no further.

My neck was being squeezed. I'd been lassoed from behind. Max had come down from his hanging place and stuck the noose around my neck. My airway was closing. I could feel the strands of the rope dig in. I gasped for air, but all oxygen was lost and blackness was coming.

"Go. Get out of here," I tried to scream to Dawn through a choking windpipe but it came out as gurgles. My hands grasped at the rope trying to loosen it to give myself time, and I could feel the mask of sanity gone now. Dawn was out of her sleep and would see me for who I truly was—more insane than all of them.

"*Go, Dawn, go,*" I tried to say but couldn't speak clearly.

She sat up, slowly as if it were a Sunday morning, and lifted herself to sit against the headboard. She gazed about the room, no trace of shock or alarm on her face.

Just before I faded to black, the noose was loosened. *Relief.* I gasped for air. Everyone waited as I coughed and sucked in oxygen, waiting to bring the balance back. The earth stopped spinning and the moon beam sizzled. Dawn finally spoke.

"Come, sit next to me. Lay down"

I did as she commanded, and nuzzled next to her like a pup to its mother, scared of the monsters in my bedroom, confused at the world's complexity.

"You were so wonderful last night," she said, closing her eyes for a moment as if relishing in the memory, her tongue tracing her top lip. "You've been wonderful all along. I knew I was right in choosing you. I knew it. You've always been an early adopter of new medicines, especially if you think sex with the pharmaceutical representative comes with it. Don't think I don't know. I'm not the first of my kind to share your bed."

Smiles spread on the faces of the three patients who surrounded me, not smiles of joy, but smirks that mocked me as if they knew secrets of truths unspoken.

"What is this? What is happening?"

"I am sorry my friend, but there are powers here at work, and that power is Quinzapine. A conception pulled together from the best of Pfizer and the shamans of Peru. Taps into the mind and perceptions, pulls the spirit from inside the corpses and sets if free. Oh the things, the places, the life changing drug you've been giving them. They can't kill themselves, no matter how hard they try. How this will change mental health and depression. No more suicides, just endless suicide attempts."

She motioned to my dead ex-patients who were standing around the room as if she were showing off a work of art, the three of them like her own golems, summoned to do her bidding. The glow of the moon peering in from the shades paled in comparison to the glow of her pride.

"Behold," she said. "These are just my new friends. I have many more. They follow me everywhere, sometimes hacking away at themselves, sometimes trying to snuff out their life in other ways. They are tip-toeing between worlds, always stuck in limbo, never falling onto one side or the other. And I want you to join us. So here, please, take this pill." She reached for her bag, and pulled out a Quinzapine pill. She presented it to me like a priest giving communion, and I opened up my mouth without question. She placed it on my tongue and I swallowed it dry.

"You know how long I have worked to get to this moment? How many times I tracked your moves, your tendency to over-prescribe medications if the perks were just right? It did not come easy."

"Why do all this? Why?" I asked, and it did not really matter. I just needed her to keep talking and seduce me into death. She was my medusa, and I could not look away.

"We need someone like you on our team. To spread the word of Quinzapine, and it's a win-win. You've always wanted to know what it's like, to kill yourself. Don't think I couldn't see behind that mask of yours. Sure, you want to save some lives, but just as strongly you wanted to take your own. To live on the edge of madness and death like your patients do. So now let's try. We'll tie this noose up proper and hang it to your ceiling fan. Or you can slice your veins up just right. The Drano and bleach cocktail I do not recommend, but that is also an option. Just a few of your choices, of course, you may choose others."

"You're crazy as they are. And I will never prescribe your drug again. You've been using me all along. I'm done with this."

My words were met with silence, and meant little. I was alone in my rebellion against those who surrounded me, and somewhere under my façade, I wanted to be used. I was easy to seduce, and the dark visions of my nightmares did indeed follow.

I spent the next few days doing as they did. An orgy of cutting my own flesh. I whittled away at my limbs with sharp knives, and the blood dripped like gravy. Puddles formed on the floor, and the more blood spilled the more alive I felt. I swallowed enough cleaning products to fill a grocery aisle, started foaming at the mouth, vomiting acidic juices from my mouth. Each moment of trying to kill myself brought such pain it was pleasure.

It went on until I could take no more, my house turned upside down and smelling like a slaughter house. They didn't leave my house as much as disappear, slowly fading into black and leaving me alone.

I had to find something to stop this. The only way was to be a psychiatrist again. I drove into work with my head feeling heavy, like a week's long drinking binge had just ended. Even with a long sleeve shirt on I couldn't hide the cuts on my neck, the deep gouges, the purple bruises.

I had excuses for my appearance ready.

Car accident. Smashed my head against the wheel. Yes, I know, I did see a Doctor. No, it is not a concussion. Yes, I am fine, No, I do not want to take the day off.

I needed work to pull my mask of sanity back on, to go back into the world of the living.

The employee parking lot greeted me, and I waited for its familiar embrace, but instead, I saw cars unknown to me. Where were the Volvos, the BMWs, and the Honda's driven by the orderlies? I walked with head bowed through the hallways towards the elevator. Psych was on the ninth floor, a locked unit, and after the ding of the elevator, I swiped my badge eager for the door to open and let me back to the safety of my office.

With each swipe of my security badge I saw the dreaded red light blip instead of the green marking clear passage. The door would not open, and with each moment, I remembered Dawn in my bed. I heard her noises during intercourse, saw the blood drip from Lori's arms, and the squeak of Eva's wheelchair.

If I could just get inside this would stop.

I banged on the door with my fist, each smash louder than the next. The bangs echoed in my head and I expected my skull to shatter.

Finally, the door opened, and I was eye to eye with Nurse Haack.

"Sir, what is it?"

"My badge isn't working. The door is broken. Thank you."

I took a step to get inside but she blocked my passage and stood tall.

"Sir, they must have sent you from third floor intake. You should not have been left alone. I am sorry, this is our fault, let me get some help."

"I am the help, I am the attending physician, and your boss, and I'll tell you when and what I need."

She put her palm up towards my chest, and I thought of bowling her right over.

"I'm sorry sir, this is a staff only entrance."

I smiled, waiting for the joke to be over, but she seemed serious and like she'd never seen me in my life.

"Come on, let me in. I've got things to do." I tried to move again, but she stood in my way.

"Sir, I am serious. You'll have a bed soon. We are here to help you. I can see it on your skin, your eyes. You're hurting, but it will get better. I just need to get some staff to assist."

Ms. Haack was talking in that condescending, de-escalating voice as if I was a patient. I wanted to holler *don't you know who I am?* To breathe fire and scald her face right off.

Instead of words I found myself reacting with rage. I couldn't tell if my fists were hitting doors or faces or shoulder blades, I only knew that they were connecting, and I was indeed screeching loud enough to wake the dead.

It was Ms. Haack herself, helped by another charge nurse, who injected me with the Haldol cocktail (Haldol 5mg, Ativan 2 mg) I know, I've written the script more than once, but now I was receiving it as a patient, and it stuck me like a stick-pin and washed over me like a wet blanket. My eyes rolled back into my head, my body grew limp. I was still conscious but only a witness to my life, my body not in my control, my tongue a wiggly worm in my mouth unable to form words.

For the most dangerous of patients, we use not just a Haldol cocktail, but also the seclusion room.

I sat alone in the seclusion room, surrounded by padded walls. A staff member observed me through the unbreakable window on the locked door.

I recognized him, but he looked as if he was seeing me for the first time. My mask was indeed gone. Now they saw me for who I really was—a mad man. Such freedom, to have the mask of sanity stripped from my face. For a while, a short while, at least, I would play calm. Soon enough, I would be let out and I would be given Quinzapine. Then I would join Dawn's army of the unmasked, just as she knew I would all along.

Oh, the joy of the little deaths that awaited.

TATTOOED ALL IN BLACK
(inspired by the song *Black*, by Pearl Jam)

"Your time is coming. You'll be leaving soon. Come back to me if you can. Let me know you're okay."

"I'm going nowhere."

"Yes, Lara, you are, but I'll be okay if I can just hear from you. Promise."

Even in these last hours of Lara's life, I was lying. I'll be far from okay.

"I won't leave you. I'll stay here. In this bed. My spirit. Right here, in this house. Look for me in the floating dust when the sunlight slices through the shades. When your foot hangs off the bed and feels a cold caress. I'll slip in and out of your dreams and be with you always."

Closeness to death had sparked her fluid tongue. Words flowed from her lips like secrets she needed to share since any word spoken might be her last. She was propped up by clouds of white pillows. A checkered afghan blanket lay on top of her. Somber light glowed from the lone lamp, and the air filled our lungs with sadness.

Cancer air.

It was there in each breath. She exhaled the cancer, and I inhaled it in, hoping to catch the disease. But no matter how much love exists in your heart, one cannot catch cancer, and she would not be taking me with her into death.

At-home hospice, they called it, and I tended to her needs around the clock where it mattered little if it was day or night. I made grilled cheese, tomato soup, or scrambled eggs, and she took small bites and then pushed the plate aside. Awkward silence filled in the waiting. Our bedroom, with a large king mattress, bedside table, and two dressers had become a funeral parlor. All that was missing was the tall funeral director who was overly-versed in the language of condolence. Lara lay there as if in an open casket, flowers delivered from co-workers and cousins lined the walls.

"Our spirits. They will commune again," she said. I gripped her hand and looked into her hazel eyes. During the first days she had come home to die, her eyes had been red from a constant stream of tears, but today all I saw was a stoic white. Her pupils were tiny black pinholes, her body was so full of death had this been an open casket for the public to see I might have closed it. Her skin was pasty, and her ears looked alien, not human. Her nose as pug-like as the dog we swore we would buy but never did. Not after the diagnosis.

"We'll be together," I said with a squeeze of my hand. "We will. I will look for you all the days until I die, and then after that."

But the emptiness in my gut told me something different. There was no chemotherapy for the sickness I had. At the hour of her death I expected my insides to be gouged out, for our spirits had been fused together. It happened as we walked the Hawaiian beaches on our honeymoon, where the salt of the deepest oceans baptized our feet. When we lay on the surf under the dark Hawaiian sky and the universe peered down. The stars were so vivid it rained in blues and reds. Her flesh pulsed with life then, her spirit as powerful as the cosmos that looked down upon us. Promises of adventures waited on the horizon.

It was on this very bed upon which she lay dying where we'd had sex with such heat and ferocity my soul penetrated hers and melted us together. Both of us cried out for God as if to say his name in thanks. We fit together like lock and key, a testimony to the glory of our creator.

But the glory was now gone.

I watched her chest rise and fall, each breath I expected to be her last. Her hand no longer squeezed back in response to my touch. The blood flow was leaving. The warmth in retreat. When she finally closed her eyes for good, I kissed her lips, waiting for the smile to return, for her eyes to twinkle.

But there was nothing. She was gone.

I curled up next to her, wrapping myself around her like a snake, and wept. I cried. I wailed. I waited for someone to intervene and bring her back to life, but death's claws would not release. Her skin grew cold with no spirit to heat it from within. The quiet of the air hung over us. Even the cancer retreated without its host. It had done its job here. Her body was dead, and her spirit set free.

The funeral was merely a series of motions. My hands were in my pockets often, twiddling at a wadded-up piece of tissue from the last time I wore this suit. My insides burst on occasion and I doubled over in pain. People rushed to console me, so I feigned togetherness and tried to keep my insides iron. I repeated what I had heard others say at moments like these as I waited to go back home.

Lara's spirit was there waiting for me and I was eager to return.

I controlled what I could in the empty house by cleaning and organizing. I made color coded labels and filed credit card receipts. I cleaned behind the stove and under the fridge. I never stopped, unless I heard something that seemed out of place, in which case I stood completely still listening for whatever tiny messages might be hidden within. When the furnace kicked on and stirred the air, my head jerked towards the noise waiting for more. But it was just the furnace, no voices, no whispers. Cars from the street outside whooshed by full of life, but inside things were dead and lifeless. I wanted to hear Lara's spirit stir in this house, to feel the heat of her flesh next to mine, but it was as if she had never existed.

Days passed, and I kept the house in such order that Lara could have walked inside at any moment and felt at home. I bought cream for her coffee. I scraped the ice off her car.

At night, I lay in our bed soaking in whatever physical residue she may have left behind. Her body's dead skin cells still lay beneath me in these unwashed sheets, and I bathed in the remains. I imagined microscopic bugs in the sheets feeding on the last traces of her flesh.

Lara's real ashes sat on the nightstand. I would have kept her body had they let me, but cremation was her wish. All that was left of her was completely trapped inside a metallic box.

But it was her spirit I needed, and I watched and listened, felt and waited, for the spirit to show itself.

At night, I scanned the darkness. A soul as bright as hers could not remain hidden in black. In the light of day things are clear, but in the dark, you can see tiny specks of colorful light floating, flickering. They are souls, and they move, they dance, they collide. They try but are unable to make a shape. There is action and motion within the air, but it was not her. Not Lara. Night after night, she failed to show up, so I gave in to sleep and woke to a new darkness each day.

Each day was spent waiting for the night to come so I could lie in the bed where she had died. I wrapped myself in the same afghan checkered blanket, a larva in a cocoon, my foot hung over the edge. Cold air danced around my exposed flesh, teasing the tiny hairs, my limb hanging over the bedside waiting for dead hands to grasp my ankle, but the touch I longed for never came.

There is no afterlife, for if there was a spirit such as Lara could return.

I shaved little. I brushed my teeth only when the grime became too much to bear. I drank Jack Daniels and waited for the spirits to make her appear. My brain became mushy. Confused. My stomach full of acid.

Hold on. Hold on. I finally left the house to visit our favorite places. First, the coffee shop where local acoustic guitar players sang and sold their homemade CD's. Next, I shopped at our favorite thrift store where we'd sift through the aisles of clothes looking for secret treasure. All our favorite memories, but each place was dead and joyless.

On All Hallows Eve I went to an orchard where Lara and I used to pick apples each fall. A brilliant yellow sun rained down in the chilly autumn air as I filled two bags full of Honey Crisps. I carried the bags back to my car and a tiny dog poked his head out from under the bumper. He had no collar, no marks, a tiny mutt-mix. There was some pug in him, had to be, and we had wanted a pug, so I took him home. Now we had our dog, and I am sure Lara looked on with a smile. The mutt licked my face in the morning to wake me. He waited for me to sit so he could jump on my lap. There he stood guard to gaze about the house as if sensing my mission to see Lara's spirit.

Now I had help.

I set an alarm to wake me at 3:15 a.m. every night, for I've heard that is the hour when spirits safely walk the earth, and I wanted to bear witness. The alarm is cold and cruel at such an hour, ripping me from sleep into a dark world. Still, I woke with hope and looked about the shadows of the room, waiting for her to materialize at the foot of my bed, for her hand to touch mine, for her eyelashes to brush against my cheek. Still nothing. By four am, I was back to sleep.

I bought a Ouija board at Target for $9.99. I knew it was pathetic, cliché even, to expect a spirit unique as hers to show herself this way. Still, at midnight during a lightning storm (for lightning storms open up the gates of heaven and let the spirits in) I put my fingers on the plastic piece and waited for movement. A lone candle flickered. My fingers hung tense on the board, all ten of them suddenly longer, skinnier, veins bulging, muscles begging to be moved as I asked, "Lara. I need you. I need you here. Please tell me. Am I alone? Are you here? Tell me."

There was no response, just me and the dog on my lap, looking at the candle as it cast shadows upon the wall, wondering what was real and what wasn't.

I was alone.

Except for neighbors. They brought me chocolate chip cookies, spaghetti in Tupperware, always asking, "Is there anything I can do?" One woman, who spoke in mumbles so soft I could not decipher quite what she was saying, listened for hours while I told her stories of Lara over coffee. Some days she wore only her robe, the roundness of her breast teasing me, her warm heart an effective space heater for my cold life. The simple act of watching her fingers wrap around the coffee cup made me long for her touch.

We finally did touch, had sex on a Saturday morning. She understood when I drew the shades, closed the door, and kept us under the covers. I needed darkness to turn her into Lara. My eyes stayed closed as I imagined it was Lara who was beneath me when she visited each week. I cried out for God in moments of ecstasy and prayer, while the woman spoke with indecipherable mumbles I hardly wanted to understand anyways.

I was still praying for my Lara back.

Weeks went on. I ate little other than from an old, expired canister of almonds. My skin grew pale and stomach gaunt. I had sex with my neighbor, I fed my dog. I took the phone off the hook and let my cell battery die.

Without the dog, I may have never left the bed. Without the neighbor, who came over near daily, I wouldn't have talked to anyone.

Forget about her, you have me, she said, and I finally began to understand her mumbles. *Lara's gone. Be with me. Really with me. Please. Just be with me.*

Her words were spoken in the dark, between the sheets, and under heavy breaths while blood rushed through my head, and I started to realize I had lost my way. The slithering words of a seductress, a temptress had thwarted my journey to reunite with my love. She was both Scylla and Charybdis and I had crashed.

Lara was watching, and I had failed my true love.

I needed to kill the Scylla. I really did.

The steak knife I pulled from the block of wood was clean and made my hand feel powerful. I tilted the metal and watched it sparkle and speak to me. I made motions with the knife, and practiced sliding it from one side of her jugular across the windpipe to the other. She had sucked my life force away from its soul mate, so it was her who must die. I would do it in the morning. I wanted it to be painless, fast, efficient, so I practiced until my muscles remembered the motions and the real thing would simply be a repetition.

But this guaranteed nothing, and the idea that had shined so brightly faded like a drunken promise. I would be back right where I started.

I want to die and be with Lara.

That was it. Why hadn't I thought of it earlier? I would either join Lara in the afterlife, or fade away into the same black nothingness that had taken her.

The dog was fed double for breakfast the next morning and gobbled it up eagerly. The unnamed mutt looked at me with suspicious eyes while I drank from the freezer-chilled Jack bottle. It burned going down, but there was more burning to be had.

I fetched the red gas can from the shed and brought it inside. The fumes were overpowering and caused the mutt to whimper. *He shouldn't be here for this*, I thought, so I let the dog out back. I looked into his sad eyes one last time, wishing I had given him a name. *Whoever finds you will care for you*, I whispered before shutting the back door and leaving him safely behind.

The whiskey in my veins made me drunk with the passion to die. I dug out Lara's leftover pills from their hiding place deep in the linen closet— Xanax, Vicodin, even Morphine. I put equal handfuls of all three in my mouth, and washed them down with a river of Jack Daniels. Gas can in hand, I climbed onto the king mattress with such relief, and it wasn't long until the mix of pills and whiskey did their work and my brain started to swirl downwards.

Consciousness was fading. I needed to act quickly to make sure it never returned. I wanted a sure death, not a temporary fix and a *do-it-yourself funeral pyre* was the answer. The gasoline was surprisingly cold when I poured it on my chest and seemed to sizzle before it was even lit. The fumes burned my nostrils. I gagged on the gas that splashed inside my mouth.

When I struck the match, flames followed the fumes, sizzling my skin and burning down into my throat. My God! I've never felt such a rush. My body burst open and my insides were released like an explosion of fireworks. It was painless, orgasmic. My soul was set free from the charred carcass and I was born again.

My spirit soared. Freedom was had. Lara would be near.

But something was wrong. The joy of death turned to pain. I wailed like a wraith with nowhere to go. My body was as burnt as a witch on a stake, and just as dead, but my soul was still aflame. Through the fire, I saw the face of my neighbor, my lover, who had let herself inside as I had planned. Her face contorted with anguish at the sight that confronted her.

I was a body no more but felt lost, adrift in the darkness of an ocean bottom. Black jellyfish were piled on top of each other, squirming, some moaning words I could not decipher, and I feared I had become one of them.

"Lara," I cried out, praying she might hear.

"Lara, come to me."

The blobs began to take shape. Bodies of black, with nooses hung around their necks, foam at their mouths, slices and cuts on their wrists and their necks, some still bleeding, some with dry blood caked all over. One had fractured leg bones that jutted out of its skin, and I saw the marrow inside, as if he had jumped to his death. Another's skull was blown off from a shotgun blast through the roof of her mouth.

Suicidal souls, all of them. I felt it, and I was one of them.

"Lara, Lara."

Yes.

Her voice! I heard her voice.

"Lara, I can hear you, but I cannot see you, cannot feel you, cannot be with you."

My love, you were with me, and I with you. I came to you.

"No. I looked for you. I waited. I tried, Lara, but you were gone."

No. My spirit was there. I was the soul of the dog who sat on your lap. I felt every stroke you gave upon my back. I watched as you suffered and wanted you to be in peace. I then visited you and gazed into your eyes over coffee, waiting for life to emerge from the sadness. I came to you like I promised. We were together and I now carry your seed. I am the spirit inside a new body, one that was lifeless and easily occupied. Together we will have a child, so here I shall stay.

Lightning bolt visions flashed and burned inside of me. I remembered the days on the couch petting the stray mutt and feeling the life in his spine. I remembered sex with the neighbor in the darkest of rooms and the sensations of her flesh on my fingers. I had none of that now, and I felt Lara fading.

"Come back."

Silence

"Lara, come back…"

I can not.

"Why?"

Your death. Your suicide. You are a murderer now. You are forever tattooed in black. It's all you will ever hear, all you will ever be. I want none of it.

"Come back"

Too late

I would have screamed if I'd had a real voice, but instead, I was a soul forever burning. Lara was alive, somehow, and with child. She would be a shining star in someone else's sky, but mine was forever dark.

I watched as she covered the last bits of flame on my body with a blanket until the fire roared no more, crumbling to the ground next to the charred body I had left behind. My skin was crispy, the scent nauseating, but I refused to accept my mistake. That I had taken my last breath. I prayed that somehow Lara could make my heart beat again and bring me back to life.

But nothing.

Now in darkness I remain. The torment goes on and time passes. I see Lara light up when she smiles at her baby, the way she used to light up for me. She inhabits her new body as though it's a new house, making it her own. Knowing she's happy is sometimes enough to help me endure getting sucked into this black hell.

But my love has its limits. My loneliness burns, my regrets an endless fuel. I beg for mercy from this perpetual pain. I beg for Lara to come back, even if it means she suffers alongside me.

And I think I've found a way to make it happen.

If I can make her life a living hell, if I can torture her each night with a touch of the darkness that I've come to know so well, if I can cause enough pain, she will no longer want to live. She will take her own life, and join me.

My persistence is one part of me that hasn't died.

I become her new cancer, the disease I once cursed I now embrace, and it will kill her just the same. I infect her dreams with fears. I turn her waking hours into a nightmare. I splash my sea of blackness onto the brilliant star shine of her soul.

Despite how strong Lara is, her shine dims by degrees each day.

Someone else will need to care for the child, Lara can do so no longer. She is back at in-home hospice, rarely leaving her bed.

Her pupils have become black holes, her skin pasty and cold. She is unable to withstand the torment.

There is no relief but to join me.

Tattooed all in black.

THE BURDENS OF THE FATHER

Janis placed his hand over his wife's belly and was certain he could feel the heartbeat of his baby inside. Tiny signs of life beat with a *boom-boom, boom-boom* inside each swirl of his fingerprints.

Her due date was coming soon, but he already felt so close to this child.

"Go. Take your walk," Kathryn said. "Because once I cut this umbilical cord, you'll be the one attached to me."

It wasn't just her white robe that made her seem to glow, her whole aura radiated.

Janis filled his lungs with air before opening the front door to walk to the park. The outside air engulfed him like a sour pool, full of decay, and each breath Janis took contained less oxygen than the one before. The park was close to the dead sea, where the air was thick with death, but soon the nation-state would be releasing the Nu-Air, rich with oxygen, so it was worth enduring. He coughed and gagged, but kept moving, as he always does.

Before the park came in full view, he heard someone screaming a sermon to nobody in particular.

"The hooves of the four horseman have trodden! Dust from barren ground will rise with the Lord's spirit. His light will shine life into the forgotten."

The man's screeching words hung over the park like a storm cloud. His wiry arms waved in the air and spread his words for all to hear. An unkept beard grew on his face, hiding the grime of one who could clearly not afford clean water. Janis braced himself for the heavens to eliminate this man. The **No-Nanny-State** drone high above was surely being alarmed by this vagabond's brain waves and the toxic CO_2 being emitted by such a non-industrious being.

Yet nothing happened.

How had the old man lasted this long without the **NNS** eliminating him? ***Capacity to be Fruitful and Generative,*** less than null. ***Capacity for Industry,*** gone. ***Capacity for Rageful Transgressions***, high. ***Degree of***

Stagnation, beyond repair. All of this certainly put him below the null state needed to live in this limited oxygen environment.

But the man could preach: *"Disease so strong it has infected the air. The new air coming is not like the new air of old. Skies will rain down and the dead shall rise up."*

The Nu-Air was coming, he was right about that, it would be pumped through the vents at the crux of mid-day, the way the nation-state of America Redux had promised. Janis lived for this spot, this moment, right before it began, when the Nu-Air was about to start its cycle, and the clean oxygen would flow to his lungs.

"The Nu-Air is a spirit sedative," his dad had warned him with words poetic, but Janis couldn't help but crave the clean rush to his lungs. It was unlike the old air that seemed full of sewage, clogged his nasal passages and made him cough up globs of black-stained mucus.

The park full of plastic greenery was crowded with others who shared this same craving. Janis imagined his wife, Kathryn, by his side, but didn't want her glowing spirit contaminated by the ash of the dead that dusted the ground. Tiny flakes of those who had been eliminated by the NNS always blew in the wind when the Nu-Air was released.

"Don't let them know you are expecting a child," his dad had told him, "Let your child breathe at home, let him be born outside of their facilities. A home birth delays facial and cardiac recognition by the NNS database. Keep him hidden long as possible."

Kathryn was growing either an *Adam* inside her, his choice of names, or a *Noah*, her choice. Both had the sounds from a better time gone by, and a new world coming, where ashes of the dead had no longer gathered at their feet.

"Thus, says the LORD of hosts; behold," the preacher continued. *"Disaster shall go forth from nation to nation ... And at that day the slain of the LORD, shall be*

from one end of the Earth even to the other end of the Earth . . ."

Janis wished the preacher man would spew his words elsewhere. A laser strike during mid-day right would wreck this clean air moment. Elimination started with the tiniest of sparks, just an electric blink from the NNS in the clouds and then—Zap! The man would collapse into a pile of dust that stank like burnt hair. The remains of the haggard man would fall to the ground, and over the coming days, the wind would blow his ashes and mix him with others. The tiny flakes of the dead gathered on corners, on the bottoms of feet, and at times kicked up in the air to float.

"Elimination doesn't hurt," his dad had told him. "Consciousness is lost immediately. An atomic implosion occurs from your heartbeat. It takes a beating heart for them to make you implode, then we become anti-matter. Just atoms of God, just a spirit. But Janis, remember this: don't say *spirit* in public, **NNS** doesn't like that. And don't say *God*."

Janis never knew for sure if his father was eliminated due to **capacity for crime** or **uncorrectable stagnation** or some other perceived evil. His dad just didn't come home one day. "When you're in bliss, you don't want to work," his dad had warned, "and become meaningless to those in power. Spiritually free is a null state to the material world, and you are no longer of use, just a waste of oxygen."

"We must bear the burdens of our forefathers," were his last words spoken. Janis felt it was his burden to follow his edict, to keep the plants hidden and have a home birth.

His dad shared histories that he begged Janis to repeat to anyone who would listen.

"The nation is trying to erase our history of the days before the Terraform when states polluted one another, wars were fought over clean air, and air purification forests were obliterated. Gas masks became a staple of the rich. The continent had to be nu-cleared, and America Redux was born. We are all a threat to the oxygen supply if we don't produce. They feed us so we keep the machine running, but these Nu-organic meals they give us are not food. They are not nourishment; they are an opioid for the soul that starts in your stomach. You ache when you don't have it, because it's a drug."

The gaunt preacher who danced and howled before Janis clearly had not eaten in a long while. His garments were a patchwork of rags and they hung on his slight frame as if he was a skeleton. Janis felt for a second that the man was an illusion, something that he alone could see and hear. His voice was a high pitch reaching different octaves than the droll humans who sat idly around him. The No-Nanny State drone seemed to ignore the haggard man as well, and Janis watched with curiosity as he hopped about and preached. This insane man had been left to live too long despite losing his mental capacity.

"You breathe the air of the state and become the state. Plants made of plastic turn us into plastic."

Janis was one of the rogue few who had seen real plants. Touched and lived with real plants. His dad grew one unregistered with hydroponics used by underground plant growers for hundreds of years. The stem had such fresh greenness, and the bud was like a slowly opening eyelid peeking at him. As a child, he liked to caress it with his fingertip. It felt scratchy on his thumb but nice. More plants would come in its place, and Dad had grown a small bed of greenery, hidden out of sight.

"The plant releases oxygen, real and true, and that is why the state wants to control it. If all the females of the land could breathe such air, our race could start anew."

As much as he missed his dad, he resented him for being so stubborn in his beliefs that it got him killed. *You were an enemy of the state, Dad, but what did it get you? You are gone, and I have no father.* His dad had left him alone, forever. Janis saw his father only in a reoccurring dream. His dad would point his skinny finger in the air like there was an idea that Janis was missing and needed to look at. When Janis turned to look, he would be shocked out of sleep and awake again to his fatherless world.

A world full of ash.

Janis shuffled his feet across the ground and imagined the ash on his feet was his dad, come to say goodbye. Sometimes when he coughed up soot from the ashes of those who had been eliminated, he looked at the blob on the piece of tissue and wondered if it was parts of his father. Janis vowed he would never leave his child alone. He learned how to get by living within the rules of the state and doing just enough to avoid elimination.

The sound of gears shifting rumbled through the park like a soft earthquake. Janis's head felt a sweet buzz from anticipating the fresh oxygen. Gears clicked and the hum of the blower began. The excitement started with a beat in his chest and spread warmth through his veins. The new air was seeping in. Glorious, glorious! Like a return to birth! Being reborn in a pool of freshness. Janis took a breath, smiled with contentment, and the dirty preacher man began to sing.

"Thy dead shall live, my dead bodies shall arise. Awake and sing in triumph, ye that dwell in dust; for thy dew is the dew of the morning."

The air was indeed like the opiate that his dad had promised. Janis sucked through his nostrils like they were straws, and the air was an elixir of youth. A clean blast of ecstasy went deep into his lungs, filling them and expanding his chest cavity. Freshly oxygenated blood reached his brain, and he imagined it seeping into every tiny capillary, spreading fresh life into the nearly dead grey matter. The energy of the park was alive. People were smiling, softly swaying in unison. An orgy of fresh oxygen air over the next 30 minutes would be like a fantastic symphony.

If only Kathryn with child in womb could be here with him. Someday soon they would all be here.

The machine churned the air, and the aging preacher man stopped bounding about. His skin pulsed with energy, beaming with power, well beyond that of any of the humans reveling in the Nu-Air. Though he'd stopped talking, his very presence seemed to emit a sound, ascending to higher pitches, new octaves, until an aura of deep blue rays shot from his flesh. He flapped his arms as if trying to fly. Small jet streams hit Janis's cheek. Dust and ash from the ground began to whirl. Tiny tornadoes began to spin in the park.

The park became full of tiny cyclones whipping up from the ground and rising towards the sky. Everything was sucked up within them. Whirlwinds of ashes congregated in the middle of each twister. The grey ash collected and gathered, until finally shapes appeared—human shapes, like mannequins. The bodies were first faceless but after the tornado spun faster and tighter a complete being appeared inside each one.

Bodies made of ash came to life.

The first born had a face twisted in anguish and a mouth born of hunger. It snarled like a dog and turned to where a bystander stood, oblivious, her nose turned to the air to breathe, her eyes closed, and her jugular exposed. The creature bit into her neck, blood sprayed forth, and the crimson red was the brightest color in the park.

The winds whipped and a dozen more beings appeared from the ashes. Their blank eyes were grey with anguish, their skin seemed broiled from fire. Their teeth nibbled on the necks of the remaining park dwellers like eager lovers. Their teeth that of sharks, slicing through skin. Blood dripped off their lips and colored their ash-grey bodies in crimson.

Janis sat silent and stunned, surrounded by the sounds of crunching bones and screams of terror. He saw families watch their loved ones destroyed. He saw human meat become fodder. He saw a small army of ash slaughtering the minions of the state too drunk on fresh air to scatter to safety.

And from the heavens, the **NNS** drone struck down with rapid fire shots, but the laser bursts had no effect on these beings reborn without a beating heart. Creatures kept springing forth from the swirl of ashes, and not a single zap from the NNS could bring them down.

The sight made him sick, and for the first time, Janis prayed the NNS would cause instant death, that these creatures could be zapped to ash, but they were all immune, and the slaughter continued. The blood from the deaths made the new air stink.

If he wanted to live, he had to move. He needed to get home. He sprang into action, but after just one step, the aged preacher man stood before him and blocked his path. The pores of the man's skin became vast caverns. One eyeball bulged out of his socket and looked into his soul.

"You, you! You will finally know your purpose. This judgment is not just a passing notion but an action that is sweeping the cosmos."

The preacher had a shaky finger pointed at Janis, right at his heart, and he felt like an electric bolt would come not from the NNS in the sky, but from the man's finger, and it would end his life.

But it did not, and so he ran. The wind whirled in his ears. Urgency beat in his heart. The swooshing noise seemed to get into his skulls and explode. He felt in the middle of a storm front, cooler air in front of him, warmer behind. He sprinted with arms and legs blazing, and his lungs gasped for air. Sucking in all this oxygen and releasing CO_2 while he was not being industrious put him at risk of elimination, but none of that seemed to matter now for something bigger was happening. Behind him the cloud of ashes was swarming like a plague of locusts.

The wind fueled him home. He dashed the 200 yards to the front of his dwelling, yanked open the front door, and there was Kathryn standing right inside.

My God.

No.

Every fear he ever had was erased, his head emptied, his heart stopped.

Kathryn's brown hair was wet with sweat and stuck on her forehead. Her head was bowed. Her robe was red and bloody, and so was the lifeless infant she cradled loosely in her arms. The scent in the room was foreign. Foul, even. Janis coughed, and a splattering of brown went into his mouth. He swallowed it down.

There would be no crackling infant tears to announce the birth of his son. In its place was death. The silent terror of a stillbirth.

With their dead son in between, he hugged Kathryn, but she herself seemed dead with grief. She was beaten, her soul and backbone hung near lifeless in his arms. And she certainly had no idea what was going on outside their door.

I forced this at-home birth. I killed my son. Dad, why did I listen to you?

A state-facility birth in a clean, well-lit place with equipment and monitors and a perfect excision would have given him a healthy baby. Even had this infant been entered immediately into the software of the state, he would at least be alive.

Janis stayed there lost in time. Seconds passed, or maybe centuries, it mattered not, until his front door swung open and the chaos of outside came pouring in. A whirlwind of ashes and beings were sucked into his dwelling, a small group with the preacher man at the lead. The haggard man shined with energy like he was a celestial star. He stood before Janis and muttered one word.

"Son."

Janis was beaten, motionless, nauseous. The word SON hung in the air and Janis stared at the preacher in a trance. *Was he human or God? Was he made of flesh or ash?* Skinny nose, gaunt cheeks, deep-set passionate eyes. He seemed wise enough to call anyone younger than him SON.

"Son," he repeated.

Janis shook his head in disbelief.

"Yes, my dear son. You thought I had died. No lasers could stop my beating heart. We are here to start a new species and take back our land."

"Dad? That's you?"

"Yes, and you knew it was me from the start. You knew it the moment you saw me. Do not pretend you did not. And do not pretend you did not know what kind of child you were making here at home. A new set of lungs to help lead us. A new set of lungs to breathe in a new air, with a heart that is not registered, and will lead when I cannot. My lungs could not make it in this world. We needed someone new, born from a mother who breathed of the fresh, green plants. You did as I said, my son. The mindless followers who breath this Nu-Air will be destroyed, and the children such as the one born from your wife will prosper."

"Dad, he's dead. It's too late. He did not live at all."

"His death was expected, but you can give him life. He may be dead, but he can resurrect."

"What?" Janis felt his body turn from defeat to rage.

"We made this happen, you and I. We knew he would die at birth, but we can save him. Together. Channel your anger to strike me down. Kill me, kill your father. Act on that impulse. That is the way to help your savior child. Strike out against your father in rage, try and commit the ultimate crime, for we need ashes of his father's flesh, your flesh, to save him and make him one of us."

Kathryn was holding the carcass, rocking him as if bringing him back to life, but it was hopeless. Janis felt his lungs bleed and he coughed spastically.

He was done here. His life was over. His Dad's eyes said as much. Janis had been his dad's puppet all along.

Anger to murder wasn't hard. He imagined his fist smashing against his father's cheek and bruising his aging brain. He concentrated with all his might as if holding his breath and letting blood rush to his head, and then swung with the aim of killing the decrepit father, knowing full well it was an act of suicide.

His arm couldn't make impact before the NNS from the heavens struck.

His father had been right, elimination did not hurt, and consciousness of his body was lost but energy of his soul moved on. The explosion was indeed glorious, a wondrous freedom beyond what any Nu-Air oxygen could ever give him. To not have to breathe, to be one with the air and free from poisonous impurities. It was spiritual bliss. He felt like a gas emitted by the purest of plants. Just the exhale of a green bud giving birth. Inside, he cackled with tears of infinite joy.

And then he couldn't say if he saw it or felt it, but the remains of his ashes swirled in a cyclone. They whipped and whirled and spread through the air, and found their way into the airways of his infant child. Flesh of the old mixed with flesh of the new, and when his child's eyes opened, his body was not fueled by a beating heart, but by the burdens of his father.

The march of the revolution of ashes was led by a grey-haired leaping preacher and his newborn grandchild.

They called him Adam.

HOWLING FROM THE GALLOWS

I'm suspended in air, gagging for breath, three feet above the floor in this abandoned home. The noose is like a tourniquet around my jugular. I suck for air in desperate gasps, but neither oxygen nor death will come to my aid. My lungs burn with fire. My feet kick the air. I sway to and fro, dangling like a lazy pendulum. Blood gathers in my head, pressure builds in my brain. I pray for death, but there is no relief, just swaying, back and forth, ever so slightly. I try to scream for help, that I changed my mind, but I can't make words, only animal noises.

It didn't have to be this way.

If I had listened to my manager, if I had listened to that boy riding the bigwheel, if I had listened to my wife, then things would be different. Instead, I hang here, tortured by the noose that failed to do its job.

"She's nowhere to be found, move on, case closed," my manager had said six weeks earlier.

"She's not a case, she's human," I snapped back, and defied his request to close the case. I had an inside tip from an old colleague that I didn't share, and I needed to prove my instincts right as a home-based social worker, so I took the trip to Maya's House.

I had parked my car down the street. *Don't park right in front of their homes*, I'd learned that. The sound of a car door closing resulted in the inevitable peek out the window, and then feigning nobody home when I knocked. Instead, I parked down the street and walked.

"It just ain't real safe to go further," Said the boy riding his bigwheel on the desolate street.

"Why isn't it safe?" I asked

"She gets on the roof sometimes. She looks at everyone."

"You mean your neighbor, Maya, have you seen her?" I asked.

The boy had no answer, but it was clear he'd go no further. He pointed his bigwheel in the other direction, and waited to witness my next move.

"You should come now, you're going to be late," my soon to be ex-wife had said before I left. I wasn't even calling to talk to her, I was trying to video chat with my son, Drew, but she picked up instead.

"I've got nearly an hour. I'll be there. Just please put him on," I asked, waiting to hear my spousal transgressions listed first, like a juror reading a verdict. but instead, she walked the phone over to him.

Drew was a yellow belt, testing for his red belt this evening, and he had already dressed in his oversized white robe. It was clearly too big on him, a touch embarrassing how slight it made him look.

"My Man, looking like a bad-ass!" I said, and he gave me a confident smile.

"Are you going to be here on time? Can you just come now?" he asked. My heart filled with cold, brittle anger. He was repeating her words. She had poisoned his mind.

Kids always know the truth after a divorce, right? I told myself, and he would figure it out, especially after I proved my worth. How I got shit done for him. Because *I get shit done*, that's what I do. Getting it done now.

I promised I'd be there, and continued walking down Maya's street, harrowing hell looking for a soul to save.

What would I find if I actually tracked her down after all these months?

I'd seen my client Maya in so many mental states. I've stared into the void of her eyes when words dripped from her lips with helpless despair. I've seen the whirling sparkle and frenetic energy of her spirit once her depression lifted and mania took over. I've heard bizarre delusional words come pouring from her mouth.

Her bipolar disorder is persistent, extreme, powerful.

The blight on this street was doing its best to expand, a rolling black fog gobbling up real estate, like tooth decay, feeding off the vinyl sidings of houses. I walked past abandoned homes with burnt shingles and sunken porches. Menacing second story windows were like eyes watching me from above. Freshly painted homes with manicured lawns were dotted in-between. The occasional lawn ornament or garden gnome offered a friendly smile, like an antibody trying to ward off the urban decay.

The whole street was a bipolar mood swing. I wasn't just walking down Maya's street, I was walking into her mind.

I looked towards the front door of Maya's house. Years ago, during home visits, her dad answered, always with whiskey on his breath but kindness in his words. After he died in the house, Maya stayed with his decaying body and in her delusional state, she was certain the noxious fumes that surrounded her were just his soul leaving his body. She wanted to stay in the stench and breathe it all in. Neighbors complained to the police about the smell in the July heat. A wellness check followed. They took the father to be cremated, and Maya to the psychiatric hospital for a seven day stay.

Maya stopped paying taxes after her dad died, the house was foreclosed and boarded up, but she returned to it just the same.

She went to the hospital again about a year ago, this time to the massive, soon to be closed, Northville hospital, and what I heard from an old colleague who worked at Northville compelled me to visit Maya's home one last time.

"We've had elopements before," she said, "but none like this. Most of what you hear is bullshit, but I can tell some known facts. A patient came busting out from the basement—no patients are allowed in the basement tunnels—but she came from there. Why the doctor had her there, who the fuck knows, but she was a bloody lunatic. Her clothes and her skin were filthy and her face was changed. She was raging, savage, beastly, and strong. She snarled like an animal but yelled words that were clearly English about her missing daughter. She finally busted out the suicide proof windows of the 7th floor. I was right there when it happened, so don't believe any nonsense saying otherwise. I looked out the broken window and I saw her get up from the ground and then run off to the woods. The moon was so bright it was like silver sunshine. Something happened, something not right. She was just a sweet and suffering patient her first days there, having psychotic delusions that she could smell her dead dad because our bodies rot like bananas and our souls are just the fruit flies that gather. 'My dad's here,' she told me, 'can't you smell him?'"

My colleague did not remember the patient's name, but I didn't need it, because this damn sure sounded like Maya.

And would Maya return home? Of course she would, and here I was, outside the boarded-up entrance to her house and about to find out.

Three steps onto her porch, and I could peer inside. The boards over her front door had been pulled back. I was certainly not the first one to trespass inside.

"Maya, are you in there? Maya, I just want to talk."

Short pause, no answer, so I slid the board aside and stepped through the doorway.

Inside, and everything was so still, like a dark museum where ancient artifacts of her life were preserved. Everything was covered in dust that fell, ever so slightly, falling like sediment. Sunlight shafts of light penetrated the darkness.

I'm in you now, Maya, your brain, your soul, your whole life.

I worried that her dead body was here, it just hadn't started to smell yet.

"Hello," I say again, trying to sound confident. These are the kind of houses that attracted addicts looking for a place to get high, and if so, I wanted to scare them off.

There's just enough light to see the shadow self of every object. There was nobody there, so I head upstairs, with each step a creak to announce my arrival.

I'd never been upstairs before, but I felt something dynamic in the air, like static electricity. Doors were all open, little invitations to different dimension of what lay inside. I passed the bathroom and saw a mirror on the wall too full of soot to reflect any true reality.

Daylight spilled from the last room on the left, and I pushed the door all the way open. Inside was one bed frame, a dresser, and the window to the front yard had been completely busted open. I moved closer to peek outside, imagining what Maya has seen.

Glass shards remained on the rooftop outside the window frame, and the little boy with his big wheel was looking up at me from the sidewalk. I gave my friendliest wave. He took it in, and turned back down the street.

I stood there waiting. I could tell Maya had been there, so I stood still as can be, trying to sync my heartbeat with the house and sure enough, I felt a presence just at my feet.

What I thought was a pile of linen under the bed was the outline of a body, lying in fetal position, perfectly still. My eyes adjust, focus, the body lay before me as if in a chalk outline.

"Maya?"

She can't answer because she's dead, was my first thought. I got down on one knee and felt something breathing, softly, methodic, *is that the house itself, or her lungs?*

"Maya, is that you?" I asked again, and I heard her weighted voice speak.

"I'm not me anymore. Or I'm more me than I ever was."

She had dried blood all over her, but whose blood was it? The scent was like left over hamburger meat.

"Have you been living here?"

"Sometimes here, sometimes my church."

"I heard about your church. Your pastor was murdered."

"I ripped off his testicles and shoved them down his throat. I'm not sure if he choked or bled to death."

God, she was delusional. These statements usually come in the frenzy of her mania, not her depression. I felt the dust of the house start to coat my body, like the fallout of a nuclear winter, settling on me. Every apocalypse is personal, and this house had found its own.

"Let's get out of here. This is no place for you Maya. I can get you help."

"No more hospitals."

She hates them, I know this. But needs them. And medications to stabilize her mood.

"You were just in a hospital Maya. What happened in there? Please tell me."

"They put new drugs into me, not like the meds you ask me to take. Different ones. They took me to the tunnels. They said I was special, gifted, but you say I am sick. They synced me up with the moon. They were going to fix my bipolar. To siphon out the worst parts, and make the best parts boil to the top. This doctor… she did things."

"What doctor is this?

"She's a monster making monsters. Changing me to how us humans used to be, when we had to hunt by the light of the moon. She said those of us with Bipolar already possessed part of that, and she tried to give me the rest. I'm different now. Everything is like it was, but so much more."

Her voice had a depth I'd not heard in all our time together. Aged, fragile, with creaks of weakness like the hardwood floors.

"Maya, I want to help you."

"Leave me. Pretend I am dead. Go back to your son. You shouldn't have left your son to be here."

How does she even know I have a son? I never told her that.

I do need to get back. I can't be late. My wife is just waiting to document it all and share it with her divorce lawyers.

I'll get back in time.

"I want to understand what you've been through Maya. I've never seen you like this. What happened in that place? Please help me understand. I heard stories. They did something to you in that hospital. I want to know. I do."

"You're a fool. If you had to live for one moment like this, you'd not have the heart to go on living."

"Please, tell me what I can do for you."

She moved for the first time, and the house seemed to shift with her, the street realigned, birds outside fluttered to a new wire.

"There's a noose hanging in the basement… you could make it work, but I know it won't."

She closed her eyes and curled her body into a ball. It felt like the house was her womb, and Maya just the fetus, sticky with red, bloody matter. She'd always been so strong, and I could still feel her spirit, but it had become so leaden, so weighted.

And she was asking for a noose—she was suicidal with a plan. I needed to get help.

"Maya, I'm going to call an ambulance."

"Too late, You better go. Best you go out through the window because *they're here*."

Before I could ask who *they* are, I heard noises downstairs

The house had come alive, people downstairs, and it sounded like they were knocking everything over. Rummaging for scrap metal, perhaps.

"I'll take care of them Maya."

Her eyes closed, just a baby in her crib and I leave her, walking down the hallway with purpose. I move down the stairs, and then I see them. Shadows moving, ransacking through kitchen drawers, looking for valuables, metal to scrap. They see me, and I expect them to run off, but instead they take steps towards me. Knowing steps. I sensed their desperation.

"This isn't your house, you're not welcome here" I said to them, staking my ground, but they kept approaching. A pack of hyenas and I'm the Wildebeast with no path to escape.

"What the fuck you doing here?" Said one man, approaching with measured steps. I'm stuck like a new dog getting its ass sniffed. Suddenly I miss my home. I should be in my car. I want to take a giant leap out of this trap, but I'm stuck.

"Ah, that's right, you owe us money," one says.

"Listen, I don't want any trouble."

"Trouble? No trouble, you give us your shit, or we take your shit."

There would be no hero's way out when the onslaught began. I was smacked across the head with a boney fist that seemed hard as a hammer. I was punched in the gut and my wind left my lungs. I doubled over, then was on the ground, crying and begging for mercy. One final kick in the temple and I saw a shot of white lightning, then blackness.

I was out, for how long, I'm not sure, but I woke with aching head. My skull felt too tight for my brain, squeezing it like a trash compactor. I was certain my cranium was split open and brain matter stuck in the cracks. My hands had been tied to the leg of the kitchen table behind my back.

I heard voices. Mumbles. Saw figures standing over me.

"We need your pin number."

This can't be happening.

"Pin number for your ATM card. 4 digits. And just try to give us the wrong number, because we know where to find this little fuck."

The picture he held up was blurry through my eyes, but vivid in my memory. It was a picture of Drew in his heisoku-dachi fighting stance, wearing his oversized karate sweater, yellow belt wrapped around his waist.

"4 digits" they demanded again.

"5621. 5621. It's the right one. You can have my money, just let me go. People know I'm here. I'm here to help."

"Oh, you're going to fucking help."

They left and I'm stuck, but not alone. Maya was there and will set me free. I scream for her to help, but nothing, just more pain inside my cracked skull. She may not hear me, or she may not care. My fingers fumbled at the knot, but each struggle makes it tighter. I tried to scoot on the floor, but the table weight was too much

"Maya," I scream again and again.

I finally heard someone. The board over the front door was moved aside, as if a huge rock at the mouth of a cave, and sunlight comes shining in.

It's not my rescue, it's them. They're back.

Soon, I can hear their lungs inhaling smoke from a pipe and blowing it out with words of orgasmic praise. "Oh God. oh GOD" and I know its *crack*. It has an iciness to it, a sinister cold smoke that leaves their words unintelligible. I tug at the rope which I realize is just the cord from the broken shades on the floor, but made into a gordian knot.

Days passed, nights and days, different shadows when the sun rose and then set. It got hot, my shirt became wet with my sweat and my pants wet with my own piss.

I asked for water, I pleaded to be let go. They ignored me sometimes, kicked me other times. They were taking out the max money limit from my account each day.

I moved most of my money to hide from my wife before the divorce. It won't last long.

Drew was wondering why I didn't pick him up. My ex was telling him, *see, he's the kind of dad who can't be trusted. That's why I need full custody.*

This is her fault. She is why I am here, trying to save people like Maya.

What will they do with me? I wonder. *They won't kill me,* I tried to convince myself, but then I realized, of course they will kill me—*why not?*

They've done this before.

It all must come to an end soon, because my life was leaving me. I got so thirsty I wanted to bite my tongue to taste the blood. My head felt like brain matter was leaking from my ears. My face was throbbing and bruised from so many first strikes.

It felt like a delusion when the day came they both stood over me like guards passing a final judgement on their prisoner.

"Bad news, motherfucker. Your cash is gone. You got nothing. We gotta take care of you. I hope you understand, it ain't personal. Unless you got something else for us, unless you can find a new way to help. You got cash in your house? We may need to fuck up your little karate kid if he gets in the way."

The nightmare had become too much. God was cruel. There is no karma, no salvation, no justice, just these two rotting souls about to kill me.

"What kind of fucking animals are you two?" I screamed at them. "I come here to help, and you do this shit? You've got no life, none at all, but you take mine? You're pathetic."

I was spitting blood as I screamed, and they paused, just for a moment, and I wondered if I was about to receive mercy, but instead, I take another beating. Fists pounded against my head, my skull was cracking like thin ice. It was my final moment.

The house roared like a lion then. A howl as if all the pain inside those walls had finally found its voice, waiting for a mouth, waiting to scream. The ferocious snarl was followed by the shadow of a monster attacking.

The skinny man's head was nearly severed in an instant by the beast. I saw his noggin leaning on edge, waiting to fall off his neck. Gurgling sounds from his throat, gargling on his own blood, until the weight of his skull makes his whole body fall to the floor. Dead on arrival.

The beast that attacked was not finished.

The other man tried to scurry away, crawling on hands and knees, and the creature dashed towards him. It pounced on the man's chest, predator to prey. It raised one of its claws in the air, then plunged down with fury. The crunching sound of chest cavity cracking was followed by the mushing noises of organs underneath. The creature pulled its hand up and held it in the air as if presenting a trophy to the Gods above.

It was the man's heart. It had ripped it from the man's chest, and howled in ecstasy before it brought the treasure to its mouth and took a bite. My own parched mouth couldn't help but water.

I was trapped, hands tied behind my back, and was next to be slaughtered. The creature stood before me, its chest heaving, muscles raging, pulsating with power. Through the dark I can make out a face. The beast is a female, her mouth dripping with blood as if sauce on her chin.

And though they've turned a shade of red, I recognize those eyes.

"Maya? Maya…is that you? You killed them."

"You killed them!" She howled back at me. "You did this! I know how to live with men like them, you do not. They died because of your foolishness."

Her voice had lost its leaden weight, but instead hit octaves never before heard. Something ancient, something primitive. I could feel every cell of her body burning with energy, her clothes in tatters, her arms with sleek muscles, her chest heaving. Her body was that of a tiger, her eyes that of a wolf.

She's not human, she's a monster, she's a werewo…

"You think I'm the monster?" she bellowed in anger as if hearing my thoughts, reading my mind.

"No, Maya. I don't. Please, don't hurt me. I have a son. Talk to me. Tell me what happened."

"The doctor did this, you see. Now when my depression lifts, this is what happens. My new mania, this is what I am now."

"It's not possible, I don't get it."

"You don't get it? But you begged me to tell you, to show you, you said you wanted to understand. Is that still true?"

I feared to say no, so I responded with, "Yes, I do. I still want to understand."

"Then I have a gift for you," she said.

In an instant, her claw swiped at my cheek. It felt like a paper cut sting, four slices so fine and deep they didn't hurt but instead released a wave of endorphins. The blood streaming down was warm and welcomed, and I flicked my tongue to get a taste. My mouth finally found the liquid it had been begging for.

"You'll not be as strong as I am when the infection takes over, but oh, you'll get a sample. Just wait. The moon shines like diamonds tonight."

She ran upstairs then. I heard her howling to the sky, footsteps running across the rooftop like some savage reindeer, and then jumping off into the night.

I'm left, more wounded than before, hands still tied to the table behind my back.

Every wound started to throb, to pulse, none more than where Maya had cut me. Each slice came alive, four electric worms burrowing deeper into my flesh, penetrating into each capillary, spreading through my veins, in and out of my heart. My senses came alive as time ticked on. Scents came in from outside the walls of the house. I could hear the heartbeat of baby racoons living underneath the front porch. I could feel the sadness of neighbors and the sounds of their dreams. But mostly, I sensed the leftover trace of Maya's dad, the scent of his soul was clearly still there. Maya was right all along.

Power surged through my veins, my chest ready to burst. My bones crackled, expanding, making room for the muscles that started to grow. I yanked free of the cords that bound my hands.

And I was so hungry, so thirsty. I needed to eat. I needed to feed. And I did. I drank from the severed head of the dead addict, slurping the bloody liquid into my dry tongue, and then I moved on to the exploded chest cavity and fed on the exposed organs.

I had fuel for the fire in my veins.

I dashed up the stairs, down the hall and I stopped in the bathroom to glance at what I've become. Even in the dirty mirror, my eyes sparkled with red brilliance, my skull had morphed into something more primitive, my teeth had turned into hungry fangs. Everything was shifting, constant motion, and I couldn't stand still.

I ran down the hall and stepped out of Maya's broken window frame. On the rooftop, I looked up at the brilliant, shining full moon. Tiny clouds only made the silver mist seem like a shot of cocaine.

I howled into the sky to express my delight. It echoed into the heavens, and I felt nature bow to my presence.

I leapt from the roof and landed in full stride, needing to move, gaining strength with each muscle blast. *God did I need to live.* I bounded over a car, taking one step to hit the roof, another to send me into the air, and to the grass on the other side of the street.

All this rage needed a face, and I saw my ex-wife in my minds-eye. I traveled with speed down the street full of urban blight, past the garden gnomes and little boy's bedroom. I moved from shadow to shadow. Street lamps can't dim the brilliant moon glow that sparked my surge through this urban squalor, on my way to the suburbs where my soon to be ex-wife lived.

I arrived at her house. Even from the backyard, I can sense she's in bed, asleep, I know this. I can feel her slow heartbeat, her lower body temperature, the rapid eye movement of her pupils under closed eyelids.

I rip the backdoor off its hinges and step inside. The house is still at his hour of night, and I move to her bedroom. I can smell the leftover stench of sex from new lovers she has taken to bed. I feel an insatiable hunger to plunge my teeth into her beating heart.

I pounced on top of her. Her eyes open for just a brief instant, her scream cut short as my claws plunge into her chest. I rip at the red organ of muscle inside, grasping at it, twisting it, feeling it crush in my palms, trying to rip out like Maya did, but she's right—*I'm not as strong*.

God, do I want a taste, but I can't wrestle the heart free, it's too much a part of her.

See what you caused? I think, My rage only grows at my wife though she's a dead, mushy mess below me. In the puddles of her blood, I sense the DNA of the child we made, the child I loved, that she wanted to take from me in the divorce.

And that child had entered the room.

I turned to the door, and there he was—my son, Drew, wearing ruffled pajamas, staring at me in shock, in disbelief. I sensed every synapse of his brain. He's trying to decide if this is a nightmare or is this real, *because it looks a bit like Dad, but it's not, it's a werewolf.*

My heart breaks when he moves into the Heisoku-Dachi stance his karate teacher had taught him so well, preparing to fight me.

I ran towards him, thinking I can pour the love out of my heart into a hug but knowing I was so hungry and full of rage that I won't be able to resist tearing him apart. I ran like a hungry beast towards him, and thank God I didn't satisfy my tongue, but instead sent him sprawling safely to the ground while I dashed out the back door back into the moonlight.

I ran as far away as I could, howling a primitive wail, hoping there's another creature out there in the moon-filled night who knows my pain, who will answer my calls, but there is nobody.

Nobody save Maya

Maya. I need to get back to her. I took the return trip to her house on Linwood, just a salmon swimming upstream to where his new self had been born. I rushed through an avalanche of stimuli in the air, as if the silver moon light has brought it to life, scents and sounds like fingerprints rising. I make it to her front doorway, where the board has now been completely ripped off and the entrance exposed.

She's not there, I would sense her if she was, so I wait inside.

And as I wait, my strength leaves me. The energy fizzles, the raging fires go out, my veins turn from lava to cold sludge. My tongue turns parchy and dry again. I curl up on the floor, needing to rest, just a piece of old furniture, wishing I could erase the images of all that had happened.

I'm a killer. I killed her.

I see the smiles my wife had for me before our love turned cold. The joy we had. The love we made. I see Drew with his murdered mom, then at her closed casket funeral. A grief he would never shake. I killed him too. I know this.

I lay on the ground, my soul as abandoned as the house. I'm a cold and broken garden gnome of Linwood Street. My legs are pulled into my chest, my arms wrapped around them. I have only my own comfort to give, and it is hardly enough.

I'm waiting, but there's nobody coming. I'm alone, no sign of Maya and no sign of a benevolent God, for if there was, surely he would not let a living soul endure this depression, this torture.

Maya, I need you now. God, is this the pain you lived with?

I remembered some of her words

If you had to live for just one moment like this, you'd not have the heart to go on living.

There's a noose hanging in the basement. You could make it work.

The noose.

It takes so much strength and will to peel myself up from the ground, but the suffering propels me. I staggered to the basement stairs, and then start my descent.

The basement is a dark tomb, but I feel like I've been here before, a familiar catacomb maze that I can navigate. And Maya is right, the noose was there, hanging, a smiley face waiting for a head to guide its way through.

A chair sat by itself on the ground, and I imagine Maya had set it up for herself but never taken the next step. I stood on top and nothing has felt so warm as the threads of that rope as I placed my head through and kicked the chair away.

My body weight fell, the noose tightened, my airway restricted. My neck snapped and I'm suspended in air, gagging for breath. The tourniquet around my jugular is a gift that will bring death, the pain no worse than this depression

But death did not come. Hours went by, and I went on living. My heartbeat would not quit.

Instinct forces me to keep gasping for air and my feet keep kicking from the pain. It's a drive I can't stop, but it's futile. I couldn't get down, and I couldn't die.

Days seemed to pass before I heard footsteps.

It's Maya, her body spotted with dry blood like the canvas a painter has decided to ditch. Her beastly self, like mine, has retreated, but she still moves with a wisdom and strength I wish I had, but don't.

"You are a fool. You are a coward," she told me, "you, who thought you could live like I do. You can't endure the trauma, the rage, the mood swings that make you want to destroy and ravage others one moment, and then die from depression the next. You went and hurt the ones you love, didn't you? And now too afraid to live."

I try to answer, but can only gag and kick. *She'll get me down from here, she will, I know it, she has to.*

"Well, you're different now. Forever changed. There are only a few ways you can die, and the way you tried to kill yourself is certainly not one. Next time the moon is full and the beast within awakes, I'll hear you howling from the gallows. Then I'll come down here and rip out your heart."

She left me then, satisfied with her answer, leaving me in the basement tomb of this abandoned house. I hung there, swaying on the noose, waiting for the glory of the silver mist of a full moon, for the savage howl in my heart to return. Because when it does, I'll have the strength to pull myself down.

Only to face the wrath of Maya, a monster who made me into a monster, and who will end my existence by tearing out the heart that won't stop beating.

Yes, Drew, I am going to be late.

MET MY OLD LOVER IN THE GROCERY STORE
A dark backstory to the Christmas song,
Same Old Lang Syne, by Dan Fogelberg

Acid burns in my stomach. This desolate room is so quiet I can nearly hear the pink lining of my gut sizzle. The acid blazes like a blow torch, and when it finally breaks through, it seeps like hazardous waste to poison other organs. To poison my soul.

My undead soul.

I carry a dead spirit inside me. A cold, undead soul, and my flesh just its coffin.

My soul died when she left. Nothing would ever be the same. This room will never be clean. Clothes and wet towels seem to spring from the ground like weeds. Dishes always piled high. Memories drip from the walls.

How often I used to be away from here traveling to a gig, Gibson acoustic in hand and dreams in my head.

Now the walls are my prison and I'm stuck.

It started when I came home and the rooms were emptied. She had enough, and left. I don't blame her, I only miss her.

Now it's Christmas Eve and I sit alone. Another Christmas Eve with just memories in my head and the stink of my rotting soul.

Bile rises farther up my throat. I wonder when I will explode like a volcano, but I don't explode, I just burn.

I want to burst. To be blown apart. I want my body to dissipate and die and no longer be conscious of anything, just a black and eternal dreamless sleep.

Instead, I live on.

What was I now? Lifeless, not just in spirit, but in flesh.

I've sliced my wrists many times, digging for the blue with the sharpest knife in the house. I sawed at my skin ferociously, but it was just a tough piece of cheap meat—rubbery, plastic, and when I do break skin, blood refuses to spill. If I squeeze where the slice is, I can get just a few drops, pancake syrup coming from the bottom of the plastic bottle, instead of a geyser spraying the walls.

It won't work, I can't die, because I'm already dead inside.

A gunshot to the head. That will work and that is my next plan, because living is such pain. Emptiness. Shattering my skull with a bullet seems the only thing to let my dead soul escape its prison.

Tomorrow is the time for saviors, but Christ will not save a wretch like me. There will be no North Star in the sky to guide me.

It was time to go out. Not just go out, but *go out*, and go out big. This bile in my gut will be shared with the world. The acid will shoot forth and others will feel my hurt.

If I must suffer, then someone else should know this pain.

The snow was falling Christmas Eve, and I stepped outside and walked underneath. Each white drop fell from a frozen, Godless sky.

Cold car seat leather makes me shiver. My breath fogs from the frigid air. I would breathe fire and bullets soon enough.

Hiller's grocery store is open. It's a lit-up oasis in the dark streets of my tiny town. Last minute shoppers out for *just one more thing* to make the family meal look just right. Like in the commercials. The warm steam rising from turkeys out of the oven. The smiling faces in the kitchen. They make that shit up in commercials. It never happens in real life.

The electric door swings open, and I feel like a gunslinger walking into a saloon. The lights of the store make me squint. Nobody notices me. Nobody can see the dead spirit inside me, and nobody can tell I have a pistol in my waistband.

I wander through the produce section looking at fruit. Green bananas would brown and rot. Apples unpurchased would bruise and be tossed. Milk cartons tagged with expiration dates I would never live to see.

A woman leaned into the frozen food section eyeing the packs of corn and broccoli, picking through as if anyone was different from the other.

I study the hair flowing down her back. Each curl on her head looks busy, alive, vibrant. Speaking to me like snakes, mocking my misery.

She's the one. I'm going to kill her.

Time doesn't exist in that moment, the present is an illusion, the future already here, and I can see the explosion from the gunshot in the back of her head. The crackling sound of the pistol, the skull fragments scattering on the ground in a pool of blood.

Clean up, aisle 5.

I reach for my pistol. I feel the cold metal. Nothing has ever felt more real than my gun at this moment and the promise that it holds. True salvation on Christmas Eve, no need to wait for Christmas morning. It was time to ***go out.***

To make her burn.

My finger is tense on the trigger. I decide to wait. I want her to see me before it happens. One person, at least, should see the pain in my eyes. The last image flashing in her brain before her death will be my suffering.

With one hand on the gun, I touched her on the sleeve.

She turned. Her eyes flew open wide.

The face.

My memory.

Synapses shot. Memories explode instead of gunfire. My God. It is her.

My old lover in a grocery store on Christmas Eve. My soulmate.

The bile in my gut resides when she wraps her arms around me. Such love. Such joy. I embrace her back hard as I could. I feel undeserving. I try to be my former self.

I breathe in the scent of her hair, the flesh of her neck. We hold each other intimate, swaying slightly to a song only we can hear from a radio frequency emitted long ago.

She was warm, safe, and if I hold her long enough, the dead soul inside me might come to life. Hark! The herald Angels sing.

I would stay here forever but the sound of clutter and something bouncing at our feet.

Instead of her fractured skull spilling, it was her purse that spilled. I tucked the pistol deep into my pocket and bend down to help her. A blue leather wallet, a package of band aids, a small bottle of ibuprofen.

She laughs hysterically at the fallen content, not embarrassed one bit, her eyes full of joy, full of laugher. She is just as I remembered.

I breathe deeply, hoping to inhale the air exhaled from her lungs into my own.

God, I could never harm her, never. But in my self-indulgent, self-pity bullshit I almost ended her life. We are both in tears, mine sad and tragic, hers happy. It was a mess.

She was the part of me chiseled out and made into something more perfect, more divine. We met at sixteen years old. It started with a nervous first kiss and terrifying backseat sex. We took adventures, like a long drive to Cedar Point to ride roller coasters and get caricature paintings. We backpacked the Appalachian trail the year before college because we thought we were going to different schools, but changed our plans around campfires where our deepest parts were smoked out. We decided not to separate and went to college together. We traveled to Chicago to see the Indigo Girls and drove back the same night. We spent days tangled up in bedsheets eating ice cream and watching movies. I was there after her procedure. When she was hurt.

And she was there in the front row, gig after gig, in the Ann Arbor coffee shops and intimate theaters.

School made her grow practical and strong, music made me flighty and erratic. When she finally left me, I had failed out of school, and worse, would never learn.

How do you survive when your passion and joy shatters?

I stopped living when she left, because my soul was ripped out.

I thought of what I looked like to her on this Christmas Eve in a grocery store. My aged skin and tired eyes devoid of hope.

"The years have been a friend to you," I told her. "Your eyes are still as blue."

What the fuck was that? I want to snatch the words back, but then she looks away and I see something. A glimpse of disappointment, discontent, maybe? Perhaps she longs for the life we had dreamed about together but never lived.

My pistol. *My God, keep it hidden.* The safety was on. I pull my jacket down to cover the bulge. I walk with her to the checkout, me with nothing to buy, and her maybe suspicious.

The first bar we try had an open neon flashing sign on, but the parking lot was empty and the damn thing was closed. I know the place. Always a false open sign. Owner serves the morning auto workers vodka for breakfast to stop the shakes.

"Bars are closed Christmas Eve I guess," she says.

But she was wrong. There were other bars open. I know of them and go there often, where lonely saps like myself drink slowly, trying to pretend they were with family. Bringing her inside would summon men off their barstools, men whose souls were also dead. They would flash their tobacco-stained smiles. They would talk to her with whiskey spitting from their lips, and she would curtly end the evening.

"Let's get a six pack from a liquor store," she says, "PBR. In a can, of course. You got a radio. We can drink it in the car. We're good."

She always loved my spontaneity. Did she realize that she was the flame that fueled it?

Soon, cold beer from even colder metal is on our lips. With each sip a little less to talk about, bigger sips to cover the emptiness. Underneath the dashboard, heat blew at our feet. The radio was tuned to Christmas songs.

We talk a bit of old friends. We held back questions we didn't want answers to. The diamond rock on her finger but no ring on mine was obvious.

"I married an architect," she says. "He keeps me warm and safe and dry."

Of course. *An architect.* Someone who built things and didn't tear them down. I didn't ask any more questions but looked into her blue eyes which told truths.

"I'd like to say I loved the man," she said, "but I wouldn't want to lie."

She could try to lie, but I would have known. She did love him once, I am sure, but it faded and emptied. Like our beers. Like my life.

Was she asking me to tell her that I always loved her? That I felt love for her right there, sitting in a cold car with snowflakes covering the roof of my Toyota, burying us alive together. For a second, my undead soul was in communion with someone else.

On the radio, Winter Wonderland played. Unmarried lovers wanted Pastor Brown to marry them in town. The vows would be broken, but the memories of building snowmen in the meadow would not.

"You still buy records, don't you?" she asks. "Because I saw you in the record store. You were flipping through vinyls of The Velvet Underground. I almost said Hi. I heard you were traveling. You were getting gigs everywhere. I thought you must be doing well."

"Do I look well?" I ask, but before she could answer, I add, "I miss it, I miss my music, I miss my audience."

"Audiences loved you," she said, and the words strum chords in my heart.

She was my audience, doesn't she realize that? She was the only audience that mattered, but I spent so much time apart, going from small town to town, hoping for something bigger to prove to her my talent, my passion. My brain flashed back through the years, images scattered like puzzle pieces, none making sense on their own. If I had only stayed with her, instead of looking to the road.

"The audience was heavenly, but the traveling was hell."

God, this was all too much.

She knew I had enough. That I couldn't take it, so she leaned forward to kiss me. Not on the cheek, but the lips. The sound of the soft smack was frozen in the car. I waited for any trace left of my soul to respond, to be brought to life, instead of a scream of agony.

"God gives us what we need, if we just look," she said. "And I needed this, to see you. What we had together is proof of grace. Please be well and remember that. Please keep your music playing."

Acid flames in my gut. I felt that old familiar pain. Now I had nothing. Just the sight of her red brake lights as she drove away. The taste of her lips on mine would soon fade.

Snowflakes dropped from the cold God in the sky. The bile in my stomach returned, sizzling like a steak on the grill. I reached for the safety of the gun in my pocket.

Something would have to give. I can't handle life anymore, but I will certainly not harm another. She saved me from that.

Instead of boiling anger and hurting another, I wanted to die in a cold shattering of icicle tears. The gun to my own head was the answer. I needed to go. Let me out, I've had enough.

My chest heaved with anticipation. I started to pant like a dog. Lights all around me from strip malls full of people who would never know my pain. I can't take it. Can't take the coldness of life falling on me tonight. I will die if this snow keeps falling. Each flake of snow that froze my world is proof that this cold feeling is permanent. I say a prayer, softly, Pabst Blue Ribbon in my hand and empty seat next to me. *'God show me you care. Show me some warmth. Make this snow stop.'*

I had fully planned to kill myself that night, at home with as little mess as possible, but I changed my mind and spent Christmas morning alive and breathing instead. I even made it to New Year's day.

Because as I turned to make my way back home, the snow had turned into rain.

Acknowledgments

This has been a unique project for me. I've always felt writing shorter works is harder than writing longer pieces. To paraphrase a quote, perhaps misattributed to Mark Twain: "I'm sorry this letter is so long, if I had more time, it would be shorter"

I certainly could not have done it alone.

Thanks to the folks at Shock Totem, Corpus Press, thanks to folks like John FD Taff and Julie Hutchings who've helped me tremendously

Huge thanks to beta readers and proof readers, Beth Griffith, Hayla Richards, Michael Fowler, and Sharry Bronson. Thanks to cover artist Kiren Bagchee for rights to use his fantastic work of art.

Lastly, thanks to every reader who ever picked up any of my works. My hope is, if nothing else, you've never been bored.

About the Author

Mark Matthews is the author of novels such as *On the Lips of Children, All Smoke Rises*, and *Milk-Blood*, as well as the editor of Lullabies for Suffering and Garden of Fiends. In June of 2021, he was nominated for a Shirley Jackson Award. He is a graduate of the University of Michigan and a licensed professional counselor who has worked in behavioral health for over 20 years. Reach him at WickedRunPress@gmail

Turn the page for a preview of his latest novel, *The Hobgoblin of Little Minds*, published January, 2021.

The first chapter of the author's new novel:

THE HOBGOBLIN OF LITTLE MINDS

Chapter One:
KORI DRISCOE VISITS NORTHVILLE PSYCHIATRIC

Everything breathes, everything speaks, with a voice that fades but is never silenced.

Kori's dad had spoken these words in his manic state more than once, and she was starting to realize what he meant. She could feel the red brick ranch exhale in relief and give thanks as they emptied the house. For twenty-five years it had held such heavy burdens, but now all that was left was boxes of dishes and pizza crusts on a paper plate.

"I need to get out of here, Mom. You got everything done, right?"

It was a statement as much as a question.

"I wish you would leave with us tomorrow. Can't you just drive behind us?"

Kori dropped the box onto the floor with unspoken disgust. A boom echoed in the empty

room, a cannon gone off, and she hoped whatever broken glass inside would cut those who tried to open it later.

"Don't act like I'm crazy for asking," her mom said. "You leave and I never see you. You won't come, I know it. You never do."

"I'll just be a few days after you. Look for jobs for me, okay? And remember, a Vet Assistant, or Vet Technician, it's called. I'm not a Veterinarian."

Mom was fishing for a fight and Kori was used to taking the bait. She eyed the front door, the oft-used escape route for this house when the walls dripped with tension.

"And don't open this box, something broke. You don't want to get cut. I'll open it when I get there."

Kori bent down to rub Hades' neck and then reached for the leash, letting Mom know the conversation was over. The aging bull-pit was eager to go, and seemed confused by the echo of her toes against the hardwood floor in an emptied house. Like her, she remembered days as a young pup, nipping at her dad like he was part of its litter and munching on his energy.

Dad's manic energy still filled the house even though he'd been gone for years. The last time Kori saw him was just a drop-off at the porch during the divorce. She had no idea it would be goodbye. If only she could've bottled up his fantastic flurry of enthusiasm and saved it for later, sipping on it when needed—but his bizarre rages and incantations that followed were a horrible aftertaste forever poisoning her life.

Dad's sickness wasn't the only memory that haunted this house. Years ago, Hades was attacked in the backyard and left with a gash on her hind leg. Her sibling, Hercules, was less fortunate. He was found bloodied and gored, his body dead but his eyes still open, looking up at Kori in shock and surprise—*how could you let this happen?*

A coyote was the likely attacker, the vet explained, maybe more than one.
Both dogs were adopted as pups from the Detroit Animal Rescue after Dad had woken

Kori up at 5am, shaking her shoulder saying, "The dogs— *our dogs*—they're waiting for us. We need to go. Let's *go!*" Soon they were sitting in the parking lot waiting for the sun to rise and the animal shelter to open. "These are them," Dad said outside their cage. "See..these are *them*." They were part of a litter rescued from a dog fighting ring, brought home to apparent safety.

But nothing was safe in this house.

Kori understood why Mom wanted to vacate with her new husband, but Kori was ready to fight, not flee.

"Your dad can find us in Florida if he wants to, you know," Mom said as if reading Kori's thoughts. "Even if he's in one of his *confusions*, he just *knows* and will find us."

Kori didn't argue the point, but gave Mom a hug and left her in the echo chamber. With Hades riding shotgun, she drove off in the Toyota Corolla, her dad's old car, one of the many things she took ownership of after years of his absence. She wore his old flannel shirts, soaked with his scent, she had piles of his old books, read the notes in the margins. Today she was wearing his University of Michigan hoodie.

Mom was right. Kori didn't want to go with her to Florida, and still wasn't sure if she would. She was looking for answers to help her decide, and driving to find them, taking the journey she always took in moments like these.

She pulled into the parking lot of Hawthorn Center, long term psychiatric care for adolescents, and parked on the fringes. Hawthorn was only a few stories high, but sprawled out at least 200 yards, with a fenced-in courtyard, a basketball court inside, and barbed wire on the top.

Shades were drawn on all the rooms, but lights still shone through the slits on the edges. She pictured the patients huddled in their rooms at this hour, having honest conversations, topics concealed and never spoken of in front of the staff. Hawthorn Center was named after the Hawthorn trees in the area but reminded her of the places she'd been to in the past.

Troubled kids like you are sent to Hawthorn, had been the threat. Well, she'd never been sent here. Instead she came here on her own, and was going to walk through the woods to the Northville Psychiatric Hospital, built on the same parcel of land, but closed and abandoned years ago. The place where troubled adults are sent.

The place where her dad was sent fifteen years ago, then never heard from again.

"I'll be back in a bit. Less than an hour," she whispered to Hades who sat on a blanket on the passenger side. She was speckled with scars where no fur grew from the night of the attack. Her ears were now forever perked in hypervigilance, frozen that way as if waiting for her attacker to show themselves again. Kori wanted to give Hades something she didn't have—trust that caretakers who love you always return.

With car doors locked and Hades safely inside, she quickly scurried into the tree line.

Tiny branches bent against her shoulders as she walked, deciding if she should be allowed to pass. The ground was carpeted by the crunch of leaves. Her lantern dangled from her fingers as she tracked through the trees. No need to light it just yet, for the moon shined with glowing fluorescence, a brilliant blue hue.

This area was dubbed The Evil Woods, one of many legends of the area. The trees tugged at her as if trying to stop her travels, but she knew the way through. She came upon a fence, newly constructed by the demolition company. Demolition was starting any day now and the abandoned hospital was surrounded with towering machines ready to tear it down.

Tonight was the last visit.

The fence had been cut weeks ago, but the metallic fibers took all her strength to bend, and when it finally yielded, she had to dart through before it snapped back in place. Last time the metal punctured her ankle and the blood squished under her foot with each step. That hadn't stopped her from spelunking into the hallways of the hospital and the underground tunnels. This desolate place felt like a second home, one that understood her on a level her own house never could.

With each step the buildings rose before her, turned alabaster by the moonlight. She scanned for silhouettes and shapes of others who might be here. So many times she'd seen shadows dashing to and fro, never sure of their reasons for coming, but they were certainly different than hers.

Red brake lights of a car circled through the parking lot. The guard had just made his rounds on foot. Now he was back in his car, the way he does for an hour or two after he walks about. There were more guards these days, as if fearful of the extra danger once the demolition started and the hospital was ripped open and disemboweled.

It didn't stop a steady stream of trespassers. She read their graffiti on the hospital hallways, crunched over the shards of glass from their smashed beer bottles, sometimes found a lit candle from a traveler just moments before her. More than once she'd heard feigned, mocking screams of terror echoing down the hallways, followed by too-loud laughter, from those who listened to urban legends that the place was haunted. Like the house she grew up in, it could never be fully emptied of its trauma.

As she got closer, she felt the beating heart inside the brick compound go *thump-thump, thump-thump.* The past lives of the patients inside tugged at her chest. The building had its own gravitational pull and energy that radiated. She touched the brick, made one last scan of the area—no sign of life—then pulled the door handle, one of many entrances pried open over the years.

Her own entrance, her own reasons. She stepped inside.

The trapped air of the abandoned hospital surrounded her, each particle like it was alive, inspecting her skin.

Who is this intruder? Wait, we know who it is. You're his daughter. He was here for years. Please join him.

It took minutes before the air settled, before her breathing and heart moved in unison with the blood circulating through this place.

Accepted inside, Kori flicked the green Bic lighter and lit the gas lantern. Its glow brought the place to life. She'd brought flashlights in the past, but the beams felt unnatural, intrusive, making her just another security guard rather than a native of this land, someone who spoke its tongue. The lantern felt so right, evidence she was a friend, and each step she took brought the darkness of the halls into the light.

The first floor was a dark cave. Below her, the tunnels that connected these buildings were black as a tomb. On the roof was a suicide-proof deck, fully exposed to the stars, and tonight, certainly aglow under the full moon. She'd been through all the levels, breathed it all in. It filled her empty spaces, the loneliness she felt in her stomach and stuck to her spine.

To her right, she saw fresh graffiti on the wall and held the lantern to read the passage; *You Can't Scream with Your Lungs Full of Dirt* written in red bubble letters. She pressed a finger against the letter 'Y' and found the paint was dry. She'd come across wet paint often, trailing the artist by just moments.

A noise unnatural up ahead.

The quick patter of footsteps ricocheted down the hallway. Another invader. She stayed completely still, trying to hear better, but the noise vanished.

Just one person, Kori could tell, but fast and light on their feet. She waited a bit before moving on. She wanted to be alone on her last visit. She stepped softly to avoid detection, but the crunch of her footsteps on rubble broke through the silence of the hallway. The crackling noises reminded her of thin ice she might fall through if her weight became too much. She walked past a plastic chair tipped over in the hallway and imagined who had sat in it last. She stepped on a discarded hospital smock that lay on the ground as if the last of the employees had to evacuate without warning.

The lantern light illuminated them all like a chunk of the moon had been brought inside.

She came upon a rusty old file cabinet that had been dragged by scrappers but then discarded when the effort became too much. Like every cabinet she discovered, Kori had already emptied its contents, ransacking for documents then folding them up into her backpack to examine at home in the light of her bedroom, as if translating ancient scrolls. She'd found inventory sheets, psychiatric evaluations, progress notes, some of it indecipherable from stains or from doctor gibberish, but all of it fascinating. Incident reports explaining why a patient was put in restraints or injected with Haldol to calm them down; just a small written history of the anguish here, the universes of thoughts in their heads, one Big-Bang expanding into a cloud of trauma.

In all her time visiting, she never found what she really wanted—an imagined dirty manila folder with "Peter Driscoe" written on the white label—and inside would be all sorts of psychiatry notes about how the man thought of his daughter, "Kori Persephone Driscoe" every day. How he missed her and wanted her to visit. She never found it in the written word, but imagined she could feel his presence through the asbestos-laced oxygen she breathed in, or that she could hear the bipolar buzzing sound that seemed to surround her dad right before he was hospitalized.

Dad's hospital stays always seemed to come like monthly menses. The first sign was his speech. He talked faster and faster until words ran into each other in nonsense, strung along with loose associations, speeding down a river full of rapids and rushing to the waterfall. He was awake for days, drinking coffee out of the white ceramic mug Kori gave him years ago for Father's Day, *World's #1 Dad* written across. The mood of the whole house lifted, as if from a tornado, getting sucked out of Kansas into the colorful splendor of Oz.

Kori missed that feeling. It had been torn out of her gut and left a gaping hole, but she did not miss the moments when the worst of the sickness took over. She could smell the bittersweet stench of his bipolar. It always seemed to hit in the early hours, 4am, full dark, brilliant moon.

At night, Dad would impulse shop. Amazon boxes would arrive in the days to follow, left up to her to return. He would start corporations through Legal Zoom with names like "Medusa Messiah," and made a webpage image of a Medusa head, snake hair a-blazing, photoshopped onto the crucified body of a bloody Jesus. The webpage was plastered with disjointed messages, word salad like; "*Look into my eyez. Feel the message. The hizz of the snakez slithering in the apple orchards will turn your heart to stone.*"

Soon he'd leave the house to *spread the word.*

Police found him one time changing his car at an Avis because he was being followed by the Chinese. He was being poisoned. Recorded by *cameras.* Followed by *men.*

And it never lasted. It crashed down, depressions led to suicide attempts, mania to aggression, and hospitals took Dad through their locked doors. Kori and her mom waited to get summoned to one of the nearby hospitals where he stayed sometimes for three days, sometimes fourteen—but one time, at Northville Psychiatric, he was never heard from again.

She wondered if her dad felt safe here when it was open and running. If she just listened in the right spot, the message would come to her, she knew it. The noises of these hallways were the same thing she heard inside her own skull, her own inner ear. And as if the compound knew tonight was different, she could feel a thicker buzz of electric current zipping through the air. The leftover scent of suffering lingered.

One last message, one final SOS, since tonight was goodbye. Time to demolish this broke-down palace. It's not safe to keep it here, the city decided, but Kori feared little inside this place of dust and melancholy gloom, besides the random security guards with their sterilizing flashlights.

Bloggers and YouTubers loved to tell a different story about the danger here, spelunkers leaving here maimed, of hearing noises otherworldly, sounds unnatural. *I heard chains clanking, being dragged. I smelled bad breath. My legs got scratched with claws from little baby creatures who seemed like elves. They chased me away through the Evil Woods.* Each blog post trying to outdo the next one, demonizing the true hurt and sickness that used to live in these walls, bullshit easily seen right through.

Footsteps ahead.

The noise returned. This time zig-zagging for a quick dash. Someone hiding, moving from one shadow to the next. She was going to see them, and thought about calling out as she moved on. She knew the creaks of this place, knew the ruckus of high school revelers, or of couples walking slowly, hand in hand. The slow descent of the bricks settling, a bit deeper into the earth as the eons passed. She heard it all.

"Madness is but an over-acuteness of the senses," her dad had told her. "*That's Poe,*" and then he moved on to other quotes too florid to discern, the tipping point when his thoughts spilled over into a howl.

She could still hear this howl from the night he exploded into anger and grabbed her by the arm and Mom called the police. Police tasered him when he ignored their commands, but it did nothing. They passed a bullet through his shoulder. That was the only time Dad had put a hand on Kori and it rushed everything faster down-current towards her parents' divorce date. Dad promised to 'get right' in front of the judge, but instead Kori saw him only a few more times before he decompensated again and disappeared into Northville Psychiatric Hospital.

And now Kori followed in these same hallways, years later, after Dad had been discharged into a "transitionary program" because the hospital closed. They couldn't share what happened to her dad because it was PHI—*protective health information*—and Dad had refused to sign for any information to be released.

Her memory of standing in the lobby once when the hospital was open was so vague, she often wondered if her mom was lying. "You went there once, remember?" her mom told her. "I tried to give you a visit. They refused. They only let you look around, and it was too much. I have kept you *safe*," her mom reminded her. "He's gone now. I bet they helped him and he's doing fine."

Rather than constantly scan the crowd of faces at coffee shops and grocery stores looking for her dad, she came to the last place she knew he'd been. Sometimes she went up to the roof to bathe in the night air, imagining the moon and burning stars tanning her skin, but tonight she was headed to the tunnels. No other area summoned her the same—the deepest part with the biggest pull. So she descended down into the depths.

The tunnels were built to connect the many buildings, to transport staff and supplies, and to move the heat through massive piping. They were the intestines where waste travels through. No windows, low ceilings, thick moisture clung to the dust, asbestos stirred up by scrappers who'd been taking out chunks to sell for scrap metal cash. She kept walking through the remains. The lantern was more brilliant down here, but could still only illuminate a few feet ahead. Every step she craved to see Dad's face in front of her, or hear the beat of his voice, but all she heard were deep, empty echoes—the sound of her own footsteps.

Following the pipes that ran like veins along the wall gave the illusion of moving faster than she was, like running down a hotel hallway. She ran the tip of her finger along the cement wall, kicking rubble down the hallway, dribbling it like a soccer ball with her feet.

After tonight her dad's memory would be buried, a chunk of her life taken away. They were demolishing her refuge, and she might be in Florida with her mom and miss the burial.

I don't want to go to Florida, I want to stay here.

Just like these buildings, Mom was slowly cracking apart. Kori didn't blame her for moving to Hollywood with her new husband. *Not the real Hollywood, the fake one—Hollywood, Florida. Not a real person, just a fake one.* Her mom knew Kori well enough to realize, Kori may never join her. The journey to the south felt like a refugee march, while walking down these hospital hallways felt like home. With each step she took down the tunnel, she was accepted by the dark that wanted to show her things the surface could not.

As if the building came to life, a flashlight beam shined from behind her.

The sound of someone moving with speed.

The security guard. He found me. He followed me.

Instinct took over and she dashed down the tunnel, lantern bouncing in her hand. Her thoughts fast-forwarded to being caught and her goodbye visit destroyed by a night in jail for trespassing, broken promises to her mom and broken promises to Hades.

She would not be caught. The chase began.

The Hobgoblin of Little Minds
Available wherever books are sold
"As a new take on the werewolf story, it is a fascinating read, but as a deep dive into the realities of mental illness, the book is an absolute triumph."
~IndieMuse.com